She thought back t **sitting across from** ~~eating~~ **tacos.**

He'd asked questions about her life and nothing at all about the race. The way he'd listened, and that cute quirk in his left eyebrow…he seemed so genuine. The next thing she knew, she'd found herself sharing with him about why this race was so important.

And now…now she felt exposed. Maybe she could run off and leave Grady behind, literally. Since she'd shared something so personal, she needed to keep him close, didn't she? Make sure he was for real.

He jogged up to her, letting his gaze roam over her—but not in a creepy way. "You're geared up like a runner, all right."

"What? You didn't think I would be?"

"Let's just say I thought this was a test you thought of on the fly. But we'll see if you're for real." He took off then, jogging easily between the parked cars and into the center of the parking lot lane.

And Maddie just stood there and watched, too stunned for words. He should be trying to impress her, to pass her test. But instead, he'd turned her challenge around. She didn't know what to make of him, exactly, but one emotion boiled to the top. She liked him.

"Hey, wait up," Maddie called, and ran after him.

Books by Elizabeth Goddard

Love Inspired Heartsong Presents

Love in the Air
Love on the Slopes
Love in the Wind

Love Inspired Suspense

Freezing Point
Treacherous Skies
Riptide

ELIZABETH GODDARD

is a seventh-generation Texan who grew up in a small oil town in east Texas, surrounded by Christian family and friends. Becoming a writer of Christian fiction was a natural outcome of her love of reading, fueled by a strong faith.

Elizabeth attended the University of North Texas, where she received her degree in computer science. She spent the next seven years working in high-level sales for a software company located in Dallas. At twenty-five, she finally met the man of her dreams and married him a few short weeks later. When she had her first child, she moved back to east Texas with her husband and daughter and worked for a pharmaceutical company. But then, more children came along, and it was time to focus on family. Elizabeth loves that she gets to do her favorite things every day—read, write novels, stay at home with her precious children and work with her adoring husband in ministry.

ELIZABETH GODDARD

Love in the Wind

HEARTSONG
PRESENTS

Recycling programs
for this product may
not exist in your area.

™ LOVE INSPIRED BOOKS

ISBN-13: 978-0-373-48711-0

LOVE IN THE WIND

www.Harlequin.com

Printed in U.S.A.

This is my commandment,
that you love one another as I have loved you.
—*John* 15:12

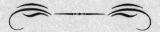

To Dan, forever.

Chapter 1

Six on a Monday morning was too early for the tourist shops in Crested Butte to come to life, but Maddie Cramer couldn't sleep.

She slipped into Desert Sea Gifts and Marine Shop, the one-of-a-kind nautical gift store where she worked, nestled just off Sandy Bottom Reservoir—one of New Mexico's largest lakes, albeit man-made. Crested Butte lay three miles from the lake and a good twenty miles from an actual butte. However, several of the steep flat-topped hills could be seen in the distance, and added just enough mystique and beauty to the desert scenery.

Maddie headed straight to the back of the store, leaving the lights off and the closed sign on the door. In addition to the usual marina supplies of tackle, rods, reels and flotation devices, the store contained the lighthouses, ship wheels, diver-helmet clocks and other nautical trinkets that tourists might find in establishments along the coast, but Desert Sea wasn't one of those.

And the small sailboat regattas in which Maddie competed on Sandy Bottom didn't compare to the sailing her father did, racing with the world's top sailors in the wide-open ocean. Maddie had been born in the wrong time and place.

She'd met her biological father—legendary entrepreneur and sailor James Carroll McHenry—in person for the first time a week ago.

Everything made sense now.

She opened the door to the employee's-only office. Tossing her bag in the corner, she slumped into the captain's chair and closed her eyes. Instead of the stuffy office air, she could still smell the salty water, feel the ocean spray against her face, remember the crinkle around her father's eyes as he smiled.

He was a member of a rich man's yacht club and had raced in one of the most prestigious of races—the America's Cup. Only the wealthy and the world's best sailors could hope to compete. Meeting him, spending time with him, enjoying a passion they both shared had been like a dream. Maddie struggled to wrap her mind and heart around any of it. Worse, coming back to her home in a little desert town in south-central New Mexico, to her little lake and little races, felt anticlimactic.

"Wake up, Maddie!"

Startled, she toppled forward in the chair, almost losing her balance. "I wasn't asleep."

Maddie glanced at the clock. Eight o'clock already. After a night of tossing and turning, she'd finally fallen asleep, all right. For two hours!

Arching a brow, Lindy Singleton smiled as she set her monster-size bag and the cooler holding her lunch against the wall. She sucked through the straw of her drive-through soda. In her fifties, she and her husband, Jack, had moved to Crested Butte, New Mexico, ten years ago to be near his ailing parents who refused to leave. Lindy had opened the shop shortly after. Maddie, who had been in her early teens, had been enthralled and had frequented the place as often as possible. She'd made quick friends with Lindy so it was only natural that she turned to Lindy when she needed a job.

Yes, Maddie had attended college in Albuquerque and had received a general business degree, but the summers were hers on the lake, and she'd eagerly returned, even after the devastating news her parents had shared when she'd turned twenty-one.

Lindy turned to face her. "You're in early."

"Couldn't sleep." Maddie stood to offer the seat to Lindy. This was her business, her office, after all.

"You're fine. Sit down." Lindy took the seat in the corner, scraping a hand through her short-cropped auburn-dyed hair. "Tell me. How did it go?"

Unsure where to begin, Maddie shook her head. "You can't even imagine."

Lindy smiled.

What was Maddie saying? Of course Lindy could imagine. Lindy came from the East Coast, from a sailing family. But she'd fallen in love with Jack, who'd moved her to Iowa where he worked for an insurance company. In New Mexico, he was just now getting involved in sailing.

"I'd like to hear just the same, if you're willing to share."

Maddie spent the next half hour regaling Lindy with her week away—the adventure of a lifetime. "And now I'm not sure if I'll ever look at the *Crescent Moon* the same."

Her J24 keelboat had been an eighteenth-birthday gift from her parents. Her very own sailboat for racing and years of sailing enjoyment. But that had been overshadowed when she'd turned twenty-one three years ago. She'd learned that Rick, the man she'd thought was her father, wasn't her birth father at all. No. Her biological father had given her up after he and her mother had divorced. When her mother had remarried, her birth father had allowed Rick to adopt Maddie, who was only two at the time, so she'd have a real family, he'd claimed. So she wouldn't be torn away on weekends like other kids with divorced families. Her mother probably wouldn't have told her had it not been for the trust fund that her biological father had set aside for her when she turned twenty-one.

But her father… He'd given her up!

The news had capsized her world. She couldn't bring herself to touch the trust fund.

It had taken her a year to get over learning the truth. Another year before she'd had the nerve to contact her biological father. And then another year, a week ago, in fact, before she could face him. Understanding why her birth parents and her adoptive father had kept the truth from her would take a long time, if it ever happened.

Forgiveness, even longer.

Lindy leaned forward and squeezed Maddie's knee. "You know, kiddo, I wasn't expecting you in today. I think you should spend some time out on the water and get reacquainted with sailing your keelboat."

"Oh, no. I couldn't do that to you. I'm here to work, if you need me."

"You have the Desert Sea Regatta in six weeks. The first regional we've had here. I know that race is important to you. A day out on the lake with your own baby, and your friends if they're around, will do you good. In fact, I insist."

"Thanks, Lindy. You're too good to me."

"No, I'm just keeping an eye on my investment."

Maddie tilted her head.

Lindy winked. "As your employer, I've invested time and energy into you. I want you to be happy while you're here."

Oh. Maddie hadn't realized how she'd come across. "I'm sorry. I didn't mean to sound like I plan to leave New Mexico. I love it here. I really do." But she'd had a few thoughts of moving out east to hang out with her father, especially after experiencing the sailing there. Her father's massive sailing yacht had definitely turned her head, not to mention the man, who had captured her heart.

"And I didn't mean to sound as though I'm only interested in what benefits me," Lindy said. "I care about you as a friend, and you're like a daughter to me." She headed out of the office to flip on the store's lights.

Maddie thought Lindy's voice sounded strained. Maybe she was uncomfortable admitting that. She hadn't shared much about why she and Jack had no children of their own.

As for Maddie's parents, they had moved to Idaho after revealing the truth about her father. They'd bought a bed-and-breakfast near Coeur d'Alene where they planned to retire early. Maybe they'd waited until they were able to tell Maddie the truth before making the move, she didn't know. But now she finally knew where her love of sailing came from, and it had been mostly genetic—it was in her blood. Nothing environmental about it, despite living near a lake.

Maddie stood and stretched, exhausted from not having slept all night. A picture of her standing next to her sailboat hung on the wall. Lindy was right. She should sail today. As grand as sailing with her father aboard his sleek fifty-foot yacht had been, there was something about being able to sail on her own boat by herself. Or even with a small crew like the one she'd need to sail the Desert Sea Regatta, which included two full days of races.

If they won this regional regatta, they'd head to the nationals. What timing that she'd met her yacht-racing, championship-winning father before this race—it was surreal.

Her five-person crew had practiced together until they were like a symphony on the high seas, only it was a lake in the middle of the desert. No matter. They were ready. Maddie's week off might have thrown their rhythm. Taylor, her bowman, had been especially upset with her for leaving. But then he went off mountain biking himself.

Maddie grabbed her bag from where she'd tossed it. Lindy appeared in the doorway.

"I think I'm going to take your advice and hit the water," Maddie said.

"Good girl." Lindy moved to allow Maddie by. "So, what about that father of yours? When do I get to meet him? I assume he's coming to watch you compete in the Desert Sea."

The thought made Maddie's heart race. "I don't know. I want him to be proud of me, but him watching me race is intimidating."

"Maddie, I'm sure he's already proud. Think about asking him, will you?"

"I have been." She strolled to the front door. "See you tomorrow."

Maddie pulled out her phone to text Taylor and ask him about getting the crew together for practice this evening.

But she already had a text from Taylor.

In Colorado with broken leg. Call me.

* * *

The obnoxious sound dived into Grady Stone's dream.

Good thing. A shark had been trailing him in the waters off Malibu Beach.

So he survived the shark, only now he was being accosted by the incessant "God's Not Dead" Newsboys ringtone. He punched the soft down pillow over his face and ears. It was early, much too early. Had to be a wrong number. Why wouldn't it just stop?

Grady threw the pillow off and bolted upright. The alarm.

It wasn't his phone ringing. Bleary-eyed, he glanced at his cell phone for the time. He had a preliminary phone interview in half an hour. Staying up much too late to fill out online job applications, he'd overslept.

If he showered and shaved and dressed for the part, he'd make a better impression for this prescreening interview, even though it was by long-distance phone call. The next conversation would likely be via videoconferencing, if not in person.

If he even made it that far.

Chances were, he'd have to move in with Aunt Sheryl who lived in Ventura, California, so he could be available for interviews in person. Candidates who already lived in the vicinity were given greater consideration.

And Grady? He was just a small-town loser since he'd lost his boat-repair business.

He drowned the negative thoughts while he dressed and prepared his mind to think positive.

Sound optimistic.

Project confidence.

Waiting for the call, Grady sat at his desk in the office behind the repair garage. He lived in the apartment above the building. Hands shaking, he stared at the phone.

This was ridiculous. He drew in a breath. He could do this. If only he could make it through the obstacles. Though his boat-repair business had sunk with the lake, he knew all about boats; he could definitely see himself as a marine manufacturer's rep, but not in the middle of New Mexico.

He'd wasted four years in college getting a degree in technical writing that he'd yet to use, but then Grandpa had died and left him the boat-repair business. Grady had always had an entrepreneurial spirit so he had taken on the business he knew. He couldn't stand to let it go.

In the end, it looked as if he would have to abandon it anyway.

Grady had hung the for-sale sign on the front door of the shop last week.

"Sorry, Grandpa," he whispered under his breath.

He'd never met anyone else who'd put so much emphasis on honor. The man had his reasons, though—Henry Kirk had served in Vietnam and kept his word to his men, had saved their lives. He was a hero. Grady couldn't hope to fill the man's shoes, but he idolized his grandfather and took everything he'd told him to heart. Understood about what it meant to be loyal and follow through with your words.

And right now, without the business, that understanding, keeping his word, was all he had left, though he'd never be required to face death head-on in order to keep his promises like his grandfather had.

With Grandpa gone, Grady felt alone in his convictions. His grandpa had gone on and on about the kids these days. Grady did his best to uphold the standard Grandpa had set, but considering he'd somehow mismanaged the business until it could no longer function, he felt as if he'd let Grandpa down. Never mind that the lake's water level was so low the marinas had closed; Grandpa had kept the business going through the droughts of the past.

Where he had succeeded, Grady had failed.

And now he would take his failure a step further and sell the business Grandpa had built. Selling the property would keep him from starving, but until then, he needed income. He'd tried to start freelancing as a technical writer, but learned quickly enough that he'd have to gain the experience on-site first. The best opportunities resided in a tech hub. Ventura would have to do for now.

Except he didn't want to leave his home in New Mexico, the life he knew and loved. He didn't want to leave his boat, the *Habanero*. If he moved to California, he'd have to pay to move the boat and then pay to park it in a marina somewhere. He couldn't ask Aunt Sheryl for more than her hospitality until he secured employment.

Lord, I don't want to sell this business, but I need to sell this business.

The cell phone rang, signaling his interview call. His thoughts had been far from where they needed to be. Grady squeezed his eyes and sent up a silent prayer then answered the call.

Half an hour later, he stared at the closed cell phone resting on his desk. He had given what he thought were great answers, but he hadn't clicked with the guy on the other end of the phone. He hadn't heard laughter when he'd injected humor. And they had both tried to talk at the same time just once too often. The rhythm had been off.

His grandpa had loved sharing clichés and idioms and had used to tell him, "If your boss likes you, you can do no wrong. If he hates you, you can do no right."

The call had been a complete waste of time. His cell rang again.

Taylor.

Grady smiled, needing to hear from his friend. A friend who had once saved his life.

"Grady, how are you, bro? So glad I caught you."

"Hey. Where are you? Still in Colorado?" Grady and Taylor had been close since that day Taylor had pulled him out of the river five years ago. They had spent summers together sailing, that was, until the drought had taken the lake last year. After that, Taylor had begun sailing at Sandy Bottom near Crested Butte.

"'Fraid so."

"Thought you'd be back in New Mexico by now training for the regatta. You made such a big deal about it." But then Grady knew why.

Taylor had a thing for a girl in Crested Butte. The guy had even gone so far as to lease a condo just so he could stay close and sail with her. He participated in sailboat races all over the country, but Maddie had caught his attention last summer and he'd stayed close.

Grady wondered what sort of girl she must be to hook Taylor like that, reel him in.

"About that. I need a favor."

Grady shifted forward in the chair. "All you have to do is ask."

Chapter 2

Taylor had broken his leg and ruined everything. Her heart went out to him, and she wanted to make sure he was okay, but what about the regatta? Everyone counted on each other to make this happen. A broken leg did not fit into the plan.

Okay, so Taylor hadn't planned for that, but what did he expect, mountain biking in the *mountains,* of all places.

Maddie fought the anxiety coiling around her chest.

She'd tried to call him back after his text, but her call had gone to voice mail. Maybe he was too afraid to talk to her until his news had settled in. *Coward.*

So she'd said a last goodbye to Lindy, hoping the woman hadn't heard her gasp or seen the complete downward spiral in Maddie's demeanor. But Taylor's words had rocked her. Her whole day was thrown now. Make that the whole month, and maybe even the year. No chance she could invite dear old Dad to come to New Mexico and watch the regatta when it looked like she wouldn't even compete.

Maddie glanced in the rearview mirror at the eighteen-wheeler barreling down on her Subaru Outback, blocking the sun from the east as she drove west until the road curved north. In the distance, flat-topped mesas turned burnt-orange as the morning aged.

Hard to believe that this time yesterday she was with her father, saying goodbye to a man she'd not even known about a few short years ago. She might never understand the choice her parents had made to keep the truth from her, and she hadn't exactly come to terms with the secret of his existence, but she couldn't stay angry despite grappling with the ache inside. And meeting him this week—her father was a larger-then-life character. She wasn't sure she fit into his world, or if she even wanted to try. He apparently hadn't wanted her in his life. But when she'd met him—all the angst and resentment burning inside her—she had seen the regret and the love in his eyes, and all she'd wanted was to spend time with him. Get to know him.

Her phone buzzed, putting an end to the cacophony of thoughts, and she glanced at its screen.

Of course, Taylor would have to text her *now* while she drove to the marina only a few miles north of Crested Butte. As badly as she wanted to respond to his text, she was on a two-lane shoulderless highway with no place to pull over. She'd have to wait until she got to the marina to read and respond.

Forget texting. She would call him again, hope he'd answer this time. But he didn't. The call went straight to voice mail again. Maybe he was talking to someone else. She needed to speak to him, and having to wait drove her nuts. She almost considered glancing at the text message, but a car in the opposite lane crossed too far over into Maddie's before swerving back. She returned her attention to the road.

Finally, she pulled into the parking lot of the marina, anxious to see her sailboat, but that would have to wait until after she read Taylor's text.

Don't worry. I'm sending a replacement.

What?
She texted back.

I'm calling you now and you'd better pick up.

Maddie made contact.

Hearing his voice, she cringed at her selfishness—all she'd thought about was herself and the regatta. "Are you okay?"

"Sure. I'm staying with my sister for a few weeks in Colorado Springs. I'm so sorry, Maddie." He sounded as disappointed as she felt. "But I plan to be there to watch you race in the regatta."

"Thanks, Taylor, but you just take care of yourself and don't worry about me." She wasn't sure she'd be sailing until she found the right person—someone who not only knew how to sail, but worked and communicated well with the crew. That would take time and practice. The crew had to click personality-wise, be in tune with each other. Read each other's minds. A person couldn't just join her crew and have everything work out smoothly. Add to that, whoever she brought on would have to weigh approximately the same as Taylor. If not, it would throw everything off, and that was the least of it.

"I'm taking care of you, too, Maddie. I found someone to replace me."

"Please, don't worry about it," she said. She would be

the one to find his replacement. After all, it was her sail-boat, and she was the skipper, as it were.

"I know how important this is to you, especially since…" Taylor sighed. "I should have asked to begin with—how did things go when you met your father?"

Taylor had become one of her closest friends during the past year, and he was one of the few people she'd shared her news with. "Listen, I'm at the marina now." Maddie stepped out of her car and shut the door. "I'll call you to-night and tell you everything. I need to clear my head first." She sighed. "I came out here to sail. Thought the crew could get together to practice tonight." But now that was off, what did she do?

"Get everyone there to meet Grady, my replacement."

Maddie exhaled. He wasn't going to let it go. "I'll be the one to decide if he can stay, okay?"

"I never doubted that."

But she'd meet him first, and then—maybe—she'd get the other three remaining crew members and they'd go sailing and see how it went.

Grady walked the pier at Sandy Bottom, a rainbow of sails splashing across the lake, the sun dipping toward the horizon. He tried not to grumble too much that Taylor had him skipping across the water like the perfect pebble.

The guy had saved his life.

They were friends.

End of story.

Still, Grady couldn't help think Taylor pushed his ad-vantage a little too far. If Grady actually had a business to run, he couldn't have simply dropped everything and driven two-and-a-half hours to temporarily move into a condo and babysit Taylor's Maddie.

Because when you got right down to it, that was really what Taylor wanted. A babysitter.

Someone to make sure that no one made a move on Maddie while Taylor was recuperating from his mountain-biking accident.

Taylor claimed that Grady would make the perfect bowman, would get along with Maddie and the rest of the five-person crew, and he wouldn't throw their weight off. The guy had begged him to drive all the way down *today* to meet Maddie before she changed her mind. Then he'd have to convince her that he was sailing material so he could be part of her racing team until Taylor was back. How could he promise Taylor it would happen? But he had to try.

Right. Grady slid a hand over his jaw.

He was there for Taylor until he had an interview or a job. At least he'd been clear on that point. With that condition, Grady would consider this his last few weeks in New Mexico. *And* he would actually be able to sail. Unlike Harris Lake, the water level at Sandy Bottom Reservoir was decent. Besides, he could conduct his job search just as easily from Taylor's condo as he could from his apartment above Grandpa's boat-repair business, or rather, his now-defunct business.

So now here he stood, pacing the pier, watching and waiting. At least now he'd get to meet the infamous Maddie Cramer, the woman who had captured Taylor's attention. Grady wasn't sure if Taylor's fixation on her was simply a matter of conquest—a mere challenge to win her over like he'd done so many other women, only to leave their broken hearts in his wake. Grady hadn't approved of that side of Taylor, but he could hope Maddie would be the one to win his friend's heart. In that way, maybe Grady would be able to repay Taylor, though, in reality, he could never *fully* pay back what Taylor had done for him.

Grady relaxed as he sat on the pier, dangling his feet near the water. He glanced at his watch. The woman had said six o'clock, hadn't she? It was well past six now, but he'd give her the next half hour if he had to. He wished he had binoculars so he could make out the boats on the water while he waited at Maddie's sailboat slip for her to return.

Sails from at least ten boats blew stiff in the wind, and then the only J24 he could make out clipped across the waters toward the pier. The wind powered the beautiful turquoise spinnaker sail, reminding him of a kite soaring in the sky. Maybe that was her. He got to his feet to see better. As the keelboat approached, he knew that it had to be Maddie. This first meeting with her could be his most important. He had to deliver for Taylor.

He'd learned that from his job interviews. First impressions could make or break success. This was it, then; he'd think of their meeting like an interview. A glance at his clothes confirmed that he could have dressed better, but then again, he needed to be able to sail at a moment's notice, and his cargo shorts would do.

The boat neared the dock and, from where he stood, Grady could easily see Maddie's trim athletic build. Taylor had gone on and on about her, sharing a few of the qualities he admired. Grady could almost believe that Maddie might be the one for Taylor.

The guy sounded possessive of her as well, and that might be a problem. Grady hadn't gotten the sense that Taylor had scored any points. Maddie and Taylor were friends, but Taylor was working to change that.

Fat chance, breaking his leg.

The boat neared the pier and Grady walked to the end of the slip, positioning himself to help. Maddie tossed the rope and he quickly moored the boat for her.

She hopped from the keelboat onto the pier, her stature

several inches shorter then Grady's. Pale gray eyes smiled up at him from a fresh, makeup-free complexion, and silky ash-blond hair fell over her shoulders. He knew anyone Taylor would be interested in would have to be beautiful, so he shouldn't be surprised.

A lump grew in Grady's throat. He thrust his hand out. "Grady Stone."

She took his hand, hers strong and warm. "Nice to meet you, Grady. I'm Maddie."

When she released his hand, Grady realized there'd been a current between them. "This the keel you're racing?"

"This is the one." She thrust her hands into the pockets of her cute white capris. Her soft blue knit top fell loosely against her form. "Taylor says you have a Santana 20."

"Yeah, it's not much." Grady gazed over the lake and nodded. "Did he also tell you I'm a little rusty? Harris Lake is way down."

Maybe he shouldn't have brought that up. He was supposed to convince her he was the man for the job, not the other way around.

"I've heard. Why didn't you just make the two-hour drive a couple of times a month so you could sail here?"

How much did he want to reveal in their first meeting? "I'm not sure what Taylor already told you, but I'm trying to sell my business. This will be my last stop before heading to California, where I plan to get a tech writing job."

Maddie studied him long and hard. Grady decided that he'd said too much and lost the bid for this position before he'd even begun. Taylor wouldn't be happy.

"Taylor talks about you sometimes. I know you're good friends. You're a good guy to do this for him."

He grinned, unsure whether or not to disclose the fact that he owed Taylor. "I'm happy to do it. It should be fun."

Truth was, he'd likely have done this for his friend anyway, considering it would be a great way to experience his last few weeks in New Mexico—a place he loved. A place where he could remember his grandpa. And what better way to do that than to get on the water again, race in Maddie's sailboat. Actually, Taylor was the one who had done Grady the favor.

Maddie smiled, briefly. "I like to have fun, too, but I'm taking this seriously, considering it's a multistate competition. The winners go to national."

"I'm here to give you whatever you need."

Maddie swung her gaze from him to the water, a soft wake from another boat rocking hers. A breeze lifted her hair from her shoulders and a few strands flew in her face. Swiping the hair from her eyes, she blinked up at him. "I have to be honest with you, this wasn't my idea. Taylor called you before even talking to me. I hate to do this, but I'm just not comfortable with this arrangement."

Stunned, Grady stared at her.

For real? Though he knew he'd have to impress her, he hadn't exactly expected a flat-out rejection with one short conversation. He ran both hands through his hair, stumbling for words. This should be something easy, unlike his venture into technical writing jobs. He *knew* how to sail. Why was this so hard?

"So if you'll excuse me," she continued, "I need to... No, wait. You came all this way and you're Taylor's friend. Where are my manners? Let me take you to dinner before you head back."

His gut churned. He'd packed his things and driven all this way.

The situation made no sense. "You haven't even given me a chance to show you my sailing abilities."

"I know. I'm sorry."

Was it something he said? Apparently she didn't like him after a two-minute conversation. She didn't owe him a thing. Not really. He recognized this for what it was. Taylor's overzealous bulldozing, something he tended to do when he was desperate. That suggested that Maddie didn't return Taylor's romantic inclinations, infatuations or whatever it was that Taylor had for her. He was trying to control Maddie using Grady, and Maddie was attempting to slip from his hold.

Man, he didn't like to be in this position.

"I won't lie to you," he said. "This is a little hard on my ego, what with me losing my business and looking for a job. I can't even get a non-paying gig doing what I know how to do? Can you at least tell me why you're turning me down? After all, I'm here to help *you*."

Not the other way around.

Chapter 3

How did she explain?

Hands hanging in the pockets of his olive-green cargo shorts, Grady looked nonplussed. Though he had a point, her decision to go another direction wasn't about him. Ever since she'd agreed to meet him, something about the whole thing had gnawed at her. Taylor had insisted the guy was already on his way, so she'd had no choice but to agree to meet him. Well, she'd had a choice, but not if she didn't want to appear rude. Now she looked rude anyway.

But she didn't appreciate Taylor's maneuverings. His tactics seemed a little manipulative, reminding her too much of the way her mother and father had kept the truth from her so they could control her life. She wanted no part of being controlled.

Admittedly, she was still too sensitive about the whole thing, even after this much time had passed, and was likely overreacting about Taylor's sending Grady.

"Look, this has nothing at all to do with you," she said. "I just wanted to make my own decision." To not have Taylor throw some guy in her face. He'd started growing pushy of late.

Grady's hands escaped his pockets and he held out his palms. "So make your own decision, but make it an *informed* decision."

Oh, he was good. How could she argue his point? When she saw the glimmer in his eyes, she knew it was more than that. He grinned, the corners of his mouth spreading well into his dimpled cheeks. Was he trying to charm his way into this? Unfortunately, Maddie wasn't immune to it. She liked it a little too much.

His brown hair looked recently cut, trimmed neat and short. Eyes the same dark color of the lake at sunset and a strong and honest face warmed her. But none of that made any difference when you were out on the water sailing in a regatta, and this, the race of her life.

"It's not so easy, you know?" Maddie gestured toward her boat. "After all, you don't train with a crew for weeks and months, building that teamwork and relationship where you can communicate with ease only to substitute the next available guy. It doesn't work like that. I can't simply trade the old guy in for a new one."

If he knew anything at all, he'd know that. Taylor should know that. Why was he so set on using Grady? On the other hand, maybe she was taking the race much too seriously. But she couldn't help it. She'd wanted so much more from it, and now she understood why.

She wished she could say that she and Grady were on different wavelengths, or that he wasn't in the same physical condition as Taylor, but she didn't know him well enough yet. What she *did* know after only five minutes with him is that his grin might be too much of a distraction.

A soft breeze cooled the heat that had suddenly risen in her cheeks.

Grady smiled. "All those are great points, but unless you have someone else in mind, why not give me a chance?"

He was right, of course. She'd only just learned of Taylor's accident, so there was no one else. There were a few friends here and there—people she knew in the sailing community—that she'd consider in the rare event something like this happened, but they were already competing in the same race, although Sasha wasn't on a crew and might be available. Maddie would contact her. Taylor had been thinking of her and here she was, acting ungrateful for his gift. Still, Grady would have to prove himself to her.

"Why not," she said, agreeing. But it would be under her conditions. Taylor was pushy and she wasn't about to give too much. No wonder she could never see herself with him. "Before you step foot on the *Crescent Moon,*" she told Grady, "let's see if you can keep up with me on my morning run."

His eyes widened. He started to say something but caught himself. She could guess what, and stifled her own grin. Was he up to the challenge? She'd make him work for it.

"You're on," he said. "Name the time and place."

"Five o'clock, Blue Mesa Apartments. I'll meet you in the parking lot."

Chuckling, he rolled his eyes skyward and stared across the lake to watch a Hobie 33 gliding in. It was Clark Nielsen. Great. The last thing she wanted was to be seen by him and his trophy girlfriend.

"What about my actual skills?"

"I already know you have those, according to Taylor, but to get that edge in any sailboat race, you need to be in top shape."

She couldn't stifle her grin any longer, and it slipped into her mouth accompanied by a laugh. Grady already had a way of making her smile. If he met her first condition, she was going to be in trouble. In the meantime, she'd make some calls, see if Sasha or someone else might be available, though the race was only six weeks from now. In that way, she could get some breathing room from Taylor. She'd find her own replacement.

Now that she thought about it, his staying in Colorado for a while could be a good thing. Give her some space.

Nielsen moored his sailboat and stepped onto the pier, followed by his girlfriend. He waved. "Hey, Maddie. Haven't seen you in a few days."

The couple headed over. "I was out of town. Got back last night."

Nielsen jammed one hand into his pristine white slacks. He was such a wannabe. He thrust his other hand out to Grady. "Clark Nielsen. This is Natasha."

Grady shook his hand. "It's nice to meet you both."

Nielsen studied Grady as if he'd quickly summed up his worth and found him wanting. Then he focused on Maddie. "I hear your bowman is out. Broken leg. Too bad about that. I guess you won't be racing in the regatta. Or… is this your new man?"

Maddie hated that he could so easily figure out her life. She hated his condescending tone. He was fifteen years her senior, and years ago he'd wanted Maddie to sail with him…and much more. Cradle robber.

But it wasn't even that. She liked to be the one in charge. Natasha rubbed up against him, tossing her platinum tresses over her shoulder. *Gag.*

"Yes, Grady comes highly recommended. He and Taylor are friends."

Nielsen rocked from heel to toe, hands in his pockets.

"I see. Well, if he doesn't work out, there's always room for one more on my boat."

After winking at Maddie and with a quick nod to Grady, Nielsen turned his back on them and squeezed Natasha to him as they headed up the pier.

"I'd figure that guy for something bigger than that Hobie," Grady said.

"Actually, that's what he meant. He has more room on his luxury boat." The thought reminded her of her father.

"Oh, I get it. So you think the guy has a thing for you?"

"Oh, please, don't even say it." She shuddered.

How had Grady picked up on the guy's vibes? It was a wonder Natasha hadn't. Or maybe she had. Fake Barbie-doll girls like that who fawned over men like Nielsen made her sick.

Grady lifted his hands in surrender. "I'm sorry. I shouldn't have said that. But if you ask me, he sounds like a bit of a creep. I couldn't picture you with him anyway."

What did that mean? Was Grady thinking about her in romantic terms? With Taylor? Or with himself? Maddie stiffened. But then Grady grinned, and she couldn't resist the way it made her light and warm inside. Yes, she'd have to make him promise not to grin. He could be dangerous that way. It had taken her completely by surprise. Maddie thought herself immune. She'd dated some through high school, but at some point in college, when she'd learned the news about her birth father, she had become a complete emotional wreck. And the past few years she'd focused on sailing and nursing her wounds.

"I don't like to talk about people," she blurted, "but Nielsen is a pretentious snob. Thinks he owns the lake." Didn't help that he was commodore of the local yacht club that sponsored most of the races.

"That's why you were quick to tell him that I was your new bowman."

Shame filled her. She'd not wanted to admit to Nielsen that she wasn't sure about Grady yet. Hadn't wanted to admit defeat to him, especially after their sailboat collision in the regatta last year for which he'd blamed her. She'd had the right of way, and he'd tried to bully her, make her cower out of his way so he could finish first. The racing committee had sided with him. She fumed at the memory.

"You okay?" Grady's question dredged her back from that awful time.

If anything, Nielsen's appearance solidified Grady's position on her crew, that is, if he could perform as Taylor had said. And outperform Sasha. And maybe even if he couldn't—because, really, finding someone at this late date would be hard, giving her few choices. But would Grady give his best? This race didn't mean to him what it meant to her and perhaps the rest of her crew.

"Don't think that means you don't have to work for it," she warned. "I can replace you at a moment's notice." Right.

The problem was she hadn't seen him in action and already she wanted him to sail with her, and maybe not just for the Desert Sea.

Grady jangled the keys in the lock of Taylor's condo, which was set in a complex just off the lakeshore. A nice place, of course. Maybe this could be like a minivacation, except he couldn't afford to take time off from the job search. When he wasn't sailing with Maddie, if she accepted, then he'd be looking for employment.

He opened the door, stepped inside and flipped on the lights. After lugging in the meager belongings he'd brought with him, he toured the condo, finding both a guest bedroom and a master bed and bath decorated in the colors and style of the Southwest.

Tossing his luggage on the floor, Grady flopped down on the bed, exhausted. Maddie had insisted on taking him to eat at the local taco joint, Taco Joe's, because she had felt guilty for giving him such a hard time. Although he'd insisted on paying for the whole dinner, she wouldn't even allow him to pay his own. She was a bit of a control freak.

She and Taylor had *clash* written all over them, even if Maddie had a thing for his friend. Which she clearly did not.

But she definitely had something to prove. To herself and maybe to others. Grady hadn't figured out what exactly. Not yet. Nor had he decided what to say to Taylor, who expected a phone call. He'd want to know how Grady's *audition* had gone.

He swiped a hand down his tired face and then began unpacking. After shuffling his clothes into a couple of empty drawers, he hung up his interview and church shirts in the limited closet space next to Taylor's clothes. Grady found a place to put his toiletries in the bathroom, and then took a long, hot shower. Though he'd already put off calling Taylor long enough, he sat in the living room and surfed for something to watch on the wide-screen TV. But nothing drew his attention away from the fact that he needed to call his friend.

He sat forward in the chair, and that was when he spotted a framed picture of Maddie on the near-empty bookshelf. Almost as if the shelf had been purchased for the sole purpose of displaying her image. Grady stood and walked over to get a closer look. He picked up the picture and held it in the light.

Great shot of her. He rubbed his thumb over her smile. She hadn't given him this one yet, and why would she?

She didn't seem to trust people easily. He'd have to work on that, but the thought made him uneasy. She probably didn't know why Taylor had asked Grady to fill in for him as his bowman. He wasn't exactly sure if there was a problem with a guy watching out for a bro's girl while he wasn't around. It wasn't exactly black-and-white, more like a gray-area thing.

When his cell rang, he jumped and almost dropped the picture. Grady set it back exactly how he'd found it. Didn't need Taylor thinking he was ogling his girl, though she wasn't Taylor's by a long shot.

Grady answered on the second ring. "Yo."

"Well?"

"I have to run with her at five in the morning, and if I pass that test, then I have to show her that I can sail." Grady stared out the window at the moonlight over the lake, waiting for Taylor to express how ridiculous this whole setup was.

"Dude, thanks so much for doing this. I knew I could count on you."

Not the response he'd hoped for. He leaned against the wall. "Anytime. But if I get an interview, I'll have to leave—I can't afford to miss an opportunity."

"No worries. I'm sure things will work out fine."

What? Did Taylor not think Grady capable of getting an interview? A job? He rubbed his temple.

"So did she say anything about me?"

Um. No. Not really. "Come on, man, she's not going to say anything about you to me. She knows we're friends. I'd just tell you everything."

"Right. Well, tell me if she does."

"I will." Grady had a bad feeling about this. "How's the leg?"

"It itches. But at least my awesome sister is fixing me a plate of nachos."

Grady could hear Taylor's smile through the phone and almost smell those nachos piled high with chili beans, ground taco beef and smothered in cheese and lots of jalapeño peppers.

"Well, I have to be up before dawn," Grady said. "So I'll talk to you later."

"Tomorrow. Talk to me tomorrow."

"How about I call you if there's anything to tell?"

"Oh, sure, sorry. But just let me know how you do on the run. I'm sorry she's being such a pain. I told her earlier tonight to go easy on you."

"So you already knew?"

"Not about the run, no. But I think you're a shoo-in like I knew you would be. She said she likes you."

She likes me? His heart jumped at the news. An unfortunate hint into his traitorous thoughts.

"And that's why you're perfect, Grady. You're the only guy in the world I could trust to do this."

After Grady said goodbye, he climbed into Taylor's bed and stared at the darkness, Taylor's last words echoing in his thoughts. The problem was, this wasn't going to be so easy. Grady couldn't get Maddie's pretty face out of his mind.

He'd never been serious about a girl before. Never been in love. He wasn't sure why, except maybe he had always been busy working at his grandpa's boat-repair shop, and the kind of girl he would one day like to marry hadn't crossed his path. No sense in dating someone unless he thought there might be a future. He trusted God to bring that person when the time was right.

Now definitely wasn't the right time, and he definitely couldn't have a future with Maddie, because Taylor wanted a future with her. If only the fire in her striking eyes and her beautiful and determined demeanor would leave him alone. The shower had done nothing to wash away the scent of the lake and sunshine and wind that had clung to her, and now to him.

Taylor's words clashed against Grady's thoughts and images of Maddie. Against Grady's loyalty, the very thing he'd prided himself in. *God, please let me get a job this week so Maddie will have time to find a replacement.*

That is, if she chose Grady to sail with her. Last night, after she'd told him the story about her father and how important this race was to her, he could no more let her down than he could let Taylor down.

He smashed the pillow over his head, wishing it would drown out the noise clamoring in his mind. Tomorrow Grady had to drag himself out of bed at a crazy hour because some insane sailboat-racing woman thought that was the best time of day to run. What had he gotten himself into?

Chapter 4

Maddie's alarm blared at 4:30 a.m.

Four-thirty.

What had she been thinking telling Grady they would run at five in the morning? She'd meant to challenge him and ended up testing herself. She might go for breakfast before dawn, but running, not so much.

She slammed the alarm off with her palm and spread out in the bed, unwilling to drag herself away from the soft pillow-top mattress. But if Grady ended up waiting for her, then she'd look the fool she was. That was enough to make her sit up.

Like a zombie, she rolled to the edge and righted herself. Made it to the shower, something she usually didn't do before she ran. That's right. She'd shower before running with Grady, though. At four thirty-five. She wasn't exactly sure why. But something told her she wanted to show up bright and perky for this guy.

The reasons she wanted him to work hard to earn his way into her private sailing club were starting to get murky. After all, work him too hard and he might just bail on her. She needed him to give his best. How did she motivate him to want to go the distance?

One sixteen-ounce mug of coffee later and she still didn't have a clue. Her running shoes and reflective wear donned, she bounded down the steps of her second-story apartment into a parking lot illuminated by a few security lights. Twilight wouldn't show for another half hour, if that.

The temperatures were in the fifties at this hour, and Maddie jogged in place to warm up, and to loosen her tight muscles while she scanned the place for any sign of Grady. Don't tell her he'd given up already? And if he was late, she'd have to jog without him, because she'd given him the impression this was her regimen. Not something she looked forward to in the predawn hours. If Taylor interfered and set Grady straight about Maddie's jogging habits, then the joke was on her.

She hated when people manipulated her, and here she was doing that exact thing to Grady.

She glanced at her watch. Only two minutes past five. She'd give Grady three more minutes. And then what? She'd made a few phone calls last night, and Grady was beginning to look like her only choice. She wanted him to work out, and yet part of her didn't. That would mean Taylor had won. Poor Taylor—he didn't even know she'd relegated him to this particular competition. He was only trying to help replace himself. But he should trust her to make the call.

She thought back to last night, of Grady sitting across from her in the booth eating tacos. He had asked questions about her life, but nothing at all about the race. The way he listened, and that cute quirk in his left eyebrow—he seemed so genuine. The next thing she knew, she found herself sharing with him about why this race was so important. About discovering that the father she'd known and loved her whole life, the father who'd raised her, wasn't her biological father after all.

About meeting her birth father who sailed amazing yachts in the expansive ocean.

The whole of it. It had taken her months to tell Taylor about her father and it had taken her only a few hours after meeting Grady to share with him.

And now... Now she felt exposed. Maybe she could run off and leave Grady behind, literally. Though since she'd shared something so personal, she needed to keep him close, didn't she? Make sure he was for real.

A car door shut. Maddie stood at attention, remembering her surroundings. And Grady, he was now ten minutes late.

"Hey!" he called. The door she'd heard must have been his.

"You're late." She kept her voice down. Nothing she hated worse than noisy neighbors waking her too early.

He jogged up, letting his gaze roam over her—but not in a creepy way. "You're geared up like a runner, all right."

"What? You didn't think I would be?"

"Let's just say I thought this was a test you thought of on the fly. But we'll see if you're for real." He took off then, jogging easily between the parked cars and into the center of the parking lot lane.

And Maddie just stood there and watched, too stunned for words. He should be trying to impress her, to pass her test. But instead, he'd turned her challenge around. She didn't know what to make of him exactly, but one emotion boiled to the top. She liked him.

"Hey, wait up," Maddie called, and ran after him.

Once beside him, she wondered about his long legs. She'd hoped to show him up, but how would she keep pace with him without lengthening her stride too much? That would do her in at the end.

"You're sure this is a requirement," he stated, rather than asked.

He'd slowed up his pace considerably, she knew, to run beside her. Speed was one thing, but distance quite another. And that was the real question—could he go the distance?

"Maybe not to some, but I'll be up front with you. I have another possible candidate. I need to make a decision. So give it your best shot and we'll go from there."

The streets quiet and empty, they ran to the corner of Maine and Temple, Desert Sea Gifts across the way, and turned right. Most of the time, Maddie liked to run along the lakeshore at a decent hour, but this morning's goal was to make it to the lake and back. Unfortunately, Grady was breathing a little hard compared to her, and they'd only run a mile and a half.

She should be gloating, but disappointment tumbled over her. She wanted Grady to be the one, except for one thing—if only Taylor hadn't been the person to pick Grady and force him on her. She was the skipper of her own boat, her own crew. Not Taylor.

They came up on a gas station open for business. "You didn't bring water, so I'm guessing we're circling around," he said.

This was off her routine and path, so she hadn't exactly thought that through herself. "Actually, why don't we run to the lake, if you're up for that." Make it sound like she'd only just thought of it.

"Sure, but let me grab a bottle of water inside the gas station, okay?"

"Me, too." Fortunately, She always carried ID and a

credit card along with her cell tucked in the zipper pockets of her shirt and shorts.

After their purchases, they stood outside and drank the water, an unplanned running break. Funny, she hadn't made Taylor go through this before he could be on her crew, but of course, their relationship had developed over time, and they'd grown together sailing on her boat. She watched Grady chugging his water and studied his lithe athletic form. He might actually look better than Taylor, but he hadn't been training to race, and wasn't in as good shape. She could tell that already. Could she dismiss him just because she didn't like Taylor's controlling ways? No. She'd make an informed decision, just like Grady had suggested.

"You ready?" She didn't want to give him a chance to catch his breath too much. "We're not stopping until we get to the lake this time."

I can do this. I can do this.

For the next several miles, Grady maintained even and steady breathing, along with his mantra. Determined to see this through, he would finish it. And he might just have to kill Taylor for arranging the whole crazy scheme. Maddie didn't sound interested in Taylor romantically, so it was pointless anyway.

Except the girl needed a bowman for this race that was so important to her.

Somewhere along the way, twilight broke through the early morning sky, turning it a pewter-gray, then purple. As the purplish hues grew brighter, the temperature rose, but at this pace, they should be back at the apartment by six or six-thirty, before it became too hot. That was the only good thing about running this early. Grady would count his blessings. Maybe he'd do so well today that Maddie wouldn't invite him to run again.

Good.

That thought tightened around his midsection, squeezing out another thought. Maybe she *would* invite him along to run every day. Not so good. He hated running and had to dig deep to keep up with her today as it was.

But for some reason he couldn't fathom, he wanted to impress this girl, and it had nothing at all to do with owing Taylor. The problem was that he shouldn't be thinking about impressing her because Taylor had his eyes set on her. And Grady was being anything except honorable with his thoughts.

He had to do this for Taylor first, and then for Maddie. He couldn't let either one of them down. Grady had a feeling if she kept him on for the regatta, he'd have to be stronger than he'd ever had to be.

I can do this.

As they jogged along the two-way highway toward the lake—not the safest thing he'd ever done—he was keenly aware of Maddie next to him. When a car passed now and then, Grady would maneuver so that he was the closest to the road. That meant Maddie had to run along the rockier part of the path, avoiding the prickly flora of the region, but it was the only way to keep her safe from the traffic.

He noticed that she'd worked up a healthy sweat, and kept up with him, even when he bumped up the pace. He had a feeling this might be as much of a challenge for her as it was for him.

"Please tell me you don't run this road every day," he said between breaths. He knew you weren't supposed to run so fast that you couldn't hold a conversation without gasping between every sentence, but he was long past that point, and still had to return to her apartment complex and his old beater Mazda.

"No. I usually drive to the lake and run, but it's too—" She bit back her words.

"Dark? Were you going to say dark? So you don't run before the crack of dawn?" He had figured as much.

"Okay, you got me," she said.

He couldn't believe she'd admitted it.

"But plenty of people do. It's the best time, really, to beat the heat and traffic."

"I don't care about those people. I just care about you. This would be a dangerous run."

Had he just told her he cared about her? Well, of course—he cared about people in general. It wouldn't be safe for any woman, or any person, to run this road in the dark. Alone.

She was Taylor's friend, if nothing more, and he cared about her for that reason, too. But all the same, his protectiveness kicked in. Even so, he reminded himself he was only here to protect Taylor's interest. And what would Maddie think about that?

"Look, see?" She pointed up ahead. "There's another runner heading back this way. It's not such a bad place to run after all."

"Just not for you." Why had he said that? If he knew anything about this girl, it was that she didn't like being told what to do. That was the whole reason behind her testing Grady and not taking Taylor's word for it. Might as well come clean. "I shouldn't have said that. It's not my business."

When she didn't respond, he wanted to know what she was thinking, but thought better of asking. Behind him, the sun rose above the desert horizon between the silhouettes of red-and-orange mesas, warming his back. Grady hated to miss the sunrise. In one swift move, he turned to face east and ran backward.

Maddie's laugh danced around him.

"We'll be at the lake soon enough," she said, "and then we'll get to see the sunrise the whole way back."

Great, the sun in his face and eyes, blinding him.

"Yeah, but the crack of dawn is a sight I rarely get outside in time to see." His apartment above the boat-repair garage didn't afford any such glorious views.

Understanding surfaced in her pretty gaze as she glanced his way. "If you want to stop and watch, we can do that."

"Ah, but I have to pass this test." He squinted in her direction. "How am I doing so far?"

"I can't tell you that yet. I don't need you giving anything but your all right now." She grinned. "You might slack off if I throw encouragement at you."

Maddie teased him, at least partially. The test was real enough in terms of the regatta. But the way he and Maddie clicked, the easy way they'd talked last night at the taco joint and even right now as they jogged, Grady figured he was good to go. That was good news to report back to Taylor.

But not such good news for Grady's trustworthiness.

For his heart.

Chapter 5

To the lake and back to her place was almost six miles. Maddie focused on finishing the last quarter mile—the end of any race, the most important. She reminded herself this wasn't a race. At least not yet.

As the traffic of the morning increased, Grady had been protective of her, making sure that she was well away from any oncoming cars. Normally she'd find that too controlling, smothering. For some reason, though, Grady's concern for her hadn't come across that way at all. Instead, she felt safe with him when she hadn't even known she'd needed to feel safe. On the other hand, if Taylor had done the same thing, Maddie would have bristled.

Shaking her head at her irrationality, she jogged the last few steps to her door, Grady right next to her. While she was impressed with him, she hadn't expected him to fail, had she? It wasn't as if they'd run a marathon.

He stopped next to her and bent over his knees, drawing in long breaths. When he straightened, he stared down at her, his dark eyes questioning hers. She could see the inquiry loud and clear in his gaze. Lest she reveal her thoughts, Maddie glanced away and walked the length of the breezeway to cool down.

Grady did the same, and when he wasn't watching her, she took in his masculine form. She couldn't help herself. He didn't appear exhausted in the least. Just breathing hard like any healthy, normal person would do after a run. He'd proved himself stronger than she'd thought.

Then he caught her staring. A slow grin slid onto his handsome face. Why was she thinking like this? She shook off the power he had over her.

"Well." He quirked his brow. "Did I pass?"

"Let's get some water," she said, holding up her empty bottle. She wasn't ready to answer. Not yet.

She dug her key out of her pocket and opened the door. In the kitchen, she tossed him a cold bottle of water from the fridge. He caught it and flashed her a grin that sent her heart tumbling. What was with her? She'd known him all of two days now. She already suspected he might be a distraction for her, but the danger level was growing by the minute.

Even if she took her time and got to know him better—and she ended up liking him—feeling anything for him at this point in her life could go absolutely nowhere. She'd only just met her father. She had to sort all that out. She wanted to visit him on the coast again, and maybe stay longer next time. A thing with Grady, if he was even interested, would stir more confusion into her life. She had to shake off the crazy way he made her feel.

Romantic feelings were one thing, trust quite another, and she didn't trust another soul, not after what happened to her. Not completely. Even with her biological father, she was treading very carefully.

She gulped down the water, as did he, chaotic thoughts swirling through her mind and heart. He wanted an answer from her. Of course he'd passed, but maybe she was the one who needed to pass a test. Could *she* sail with *him?* Would he throw her focus off? Skippering and managing a crew during a race took extraordinary self-control and command of the situation. If Grady was too much of a distraction, he could ruin her chances of winning and impressing her father.

She set the bottle of water down. The thought of her father coming to watch her race intimidated her, but even if she invited him, would he show up? Would he cheer her on? Or was she hoping for, counting on, too much?

"Maddie," Grady said.

His smooth tone coaxed her back to the present without demanding from her the answer she knew he wanted.

"Just keep up the running, and you'll get there," she said.

He tensed, throwing his shoulders back a little. "What are you saying?"

Maddie smiled. She enjoyed teasing him too much. Maybe it was the way he reacted that made her playful. "You've earned the chance to show me your sailing chops. The right to step on board the *Crescent Moon*. I'll get my crew together, and let's see if we can work with you."

"That's all I could ask," he said. He finished the rest of his water and tossed the bottle in her recycling bin. "Guess I should head back to the condo, then. Grab a shower. Start the day. When do we meet to sail?"

"I'll call you when I figure that out." Maddie moved to the door. "I don't suppose you'd be interested in running with me every morning."

What am I doing?

He studied her like he wanted to know exactly what she was thinking. But he couldn't know because she hadn't figured things out herself.

He cocked a lopsided grin, sending warmth swimming through her stomach. "I'll have to let you know. But the truth is I hate running."

Maddie chuckled. "You did great for someone who hates it. I'll call you later."

After he'd gone, she realized just how much she'd enjoyed the run and his company. At least she knew now he could give as good as he got. Likely, that was exactly the quality she needed in the regatta. As long as he could sail as well as Taylor said. And why would she doubt Taylor? He'd likely tell her she was going too far with this. Wasting precious time when they could be training.

Taylor sailed because he enjoyed it, and if she knew anything about Taylor, it was that he was all about having fun. He didn't seem to take much of anything too seriously.

Maddie loved sailing, too, and she took *everything* seriously. She wanted something more, and hadn't known what that was until she'd gone to meet her father. His world of sailing struck a deep chord inside her that still resonated with her, here in the desert. But at the same time, the magnitude of his yacht-racing culture only diminished her own efforts. At least, it felt that way.

Maddie sighed, feeling Grady's absence more than she should. She showered and readied for a day working at the gift shop. She did a quick email check and found a message from Taylor. She'd emailed last night to tell him about Sasha, a friend that could likely sail with her and take Taylor's place, though she weighed less than him.

Taylor didn't like her idea at all, and insisted that Grady needed to be there. He gave some sob story that Grady needed to do this. Frustrated, Maddie exited the email without replying. She didn't get the sense that Grady was a needy sort of person, but rather, he was simply helping Taylor.

Maddie had already decided that Grady could sail with her, that was, if she could restrain the way he distracted her, and if he was able to actually sail. The true test would be which person—Sasha or Grady—made the right moves for weight distribution that would propel the boat forward. Her crew was already trained, so she didn't have to constantly tell them when and where to move. Too much time focused on the crew's position drew her attention away from tactics.

And that was exactly what Taylor's email was doing— pulling her attention away from what was important and pushing her in what might be the wrong direction. She was too rebellious for her own good. She admitted that.

She grabbed her purse and headed out the door to work, thoughts of the years she had missed with her father, of Taylor's bulldozing tactics all competing for her attention when she should be focused on the race.

But the memory of Grady's compassionate, midnight-blue eyes, the way he'd listened to her and the easy way she'd felt with him when they ran together this morning won out over any other thoughts.

The day that had started out so well had taken a turn for the worse. Grady swerved into a parking spot at the marina half an hour late, hating himself for taking that call. But he'd hoped and prayed he'd hear back from this company. *Thank You, God!*

But why had it come minutes before he was to leave to meet Maddie? She'd called Tuesday night to schedule Grady to meet the rest of the crew and sail with them the next day. See if they could work together. And had he been mistaken? Or had he heard the hope in her voice? Maybe he'd only imagined it, considering his own hopeful outlook.

By missing their meeting time by half an hour, Grady had let her down and likely blown his chance. He'd let Taylor down, too. He jumped from his old beater and ran down the pier past thirty boats of every size to Maddie's slip. He gasped, surprised to see her boat still waiting there for him, bobbing in the gentle breeze.

And Maddie stood there, too.

Relief washed over him, but only to a point.

He started to hop on, but hesitated when he saw the look on her face. She was alone on the boat. Just as he'd feared, he'd blown it.

"Everyone left already?" he asked. Stupid question.

She scowled, the look such a contrast to her smiles yesterday morning. Why had she stayed behind to wait for him then? Or did he have it all wrong?

Oh, he got it. She had stayed to berate him when he finally showed.

He lifted his palms. "Maddie, I'm so sorry, I had—"

"Don't worry about it. If you can't make it on time, then you're not a good fit." Hurt flashed across her pale gray eyes. "I'm going with Sasha."

What? "Who?"

"A friend of mine. I know she can sail." Maddie readied the *Crescent Moon* to take her out on the lake.

All by herself. Without her crew. Without Grady.

His stomach churned, as if he'd just been dropped from a skyscraper. He didn't want to lose this chance any more than he'd wanted to mess up on his preliminary interview with the Dynamics Corporation.

Did he really want to tell her everything? He blew out

a breath. "I had a phone interview for a job and I couldn't just hang up." There, get it out before she cut him off again. "It was important."

Well, maybe he shouldn't have added that last part. He'd made it sound as if she wasn't.

"What I meant to say was that the phone interview was as important as sailing with your crew was this evening, and that's why I'm late." If she couldn't understand that, then there wasn't anything else he could do to convince her. Exasperation weighed him down. Maybe she had become too important to him already.

She started to reach for the knot that kept her boat secured to the pier, then stopped and stared at him. Something in her gaze softened. Grady took a chance. He untied the knot and stepped aboard.

Though her eyes widened a little, he saw warmth in them.

"I…I didn't know." She took a step back. "Look, is this going to be a problem? I mean, interviewing for jobs obviously interferes with your ability to train."

Grady ran his hand up the main mast and back down over the boom, admiring the care she took with her vessel.

"Take me out, Maddie." He slid his gaze sideways at her. Could she see how much he craved being on the water? With her?

"The crew is gone already. I can't call them back." Though agitation once again laced her tone, he decided she wasn't angry with him anymore. Just frustrated with the evening, as was he.

"No, I mean just the two of us." He locked eyes with her. "Right now."

He needed to convince her to give him another chance with her crew. For Taylor, and for her—Grady wanted to help her. But it was more than that. He hadn't stopped thinking about her since their run. His heart clamored in his chest, waiting for her response.

"You understand that sailing with me isn't the same as racing with my crew, right? If that's what you're thinking." A gust whipped her hair across her face, and she pulled it away, a soft smile fighting to break across her lips.

She was close to becoming the Maddie he'd seen yesterday morning when they'd run. That was the Maddie he wanted to see now. Warm tension knotted in his stomach. Oh, he was beginning to see what Taylor saw in her, and so much more. She had a spunk and a way about her that Grady found hard to resist himself. But he had to be strong for his friend. Remain true. Maybe he should wait to sail with her crew. But he knew this could be his last chance to seal the deal. Or at least convince her to give him a second chance to try.

"Yep. I know. But I'm here. You're here. We're on the boat. Let's go sailing." Spreading across his face was a smile he felt all the way to his toes.

In return, he was rewarded with that cute tilt of her head, and a warm grin—there she was, the Maddie he wanted to see again. "That's the best offer I've had in a long time," she said.

"Now we're talking," he said.

Together they readied the *Crescent Moon*.

Grady asked Maddie for a lifejacket, which he donned. "Where's yours?"

"They're too cumbersome."

He stared her down.

"What?"

"You should always wear your lifejacket. What about when you race? What about your crew?"

"Ricky wears one."

Grady shook his head. Just a personal safety preference,

he guessed. His grandpa hadn't always worn his, either. Grady had the pleasure of hoisting the mainsail just as they left the dock. As Maddie's keelboat glided across the lake like a skater across ice, Grady's gaze followed the mainmast up to the sky. He watched it capture the light wind, the top batten running parallel to the boom.

He closed his eyes and allowed the wind to flow over him, to capture his heart once again. The familiar flapping sounds of air rippling through the sail, and the soothing whisper of water. Oh, how he had missed this.

"Earth to Grady," Maddie said.

He opened his eyes and grinned, loving this moment. Wishing he could recapture the times he had spent with his grandfather on the *Habanero.*

"I can sail this all by my lonesome, but your help would be nice when it's time to heave to." She stood in the pit.

"Heaving to?"

"Yeah, I have someplace I've wanted to go for a while. Might as well go there today."

"Where's that?"

"You'll see," she said. Her eyes shimmered with some emotion he couldn't read.

He didn't know her well enough, but he thought he saw delight in her eyes. Did Maddie like him? Or was it something else? Looking away and across the lake at the shoreline and the bluff like a sentinel over Sandy Bottom, Grady smiled to himself.

He liked her, too. Though regret rose in his chest, he shoved it down.

Maddie steered the *Crescent Moon* straight across the lake, and when they neared a small cove, they tacked through the center of the wind, heaved to and then lowered the mainsail and anchored.

Grady didn't remember Taylor mentioning this cove

and wondered if he'd been there with Maddie, as well. If not, Grady wasn't sure it would be wise to bring this up to Taylor. He hadn't even started training for the regatta with Maddie and already guilt gnawed at him—but he hadn't done a thing wrong. Yet. As long as he could redirect his heart, Grady could remain true to his friend.

Maddie went belowdecks to the small cabin and reappeared with an ice chest. She opened it and offered him a choice of sodas. He took a Coke, and she sat next to him with hers. They let their legs dangle over the side of the boat as it rested peacefully in the calm waters.

He'd never asked for perfect, but this was perfect.

He couldn't fathom why she'd brought him here. Surely he didn't rank among the friends that she would take to a secluded cove. Why him? What was she up to?

If only Taylor didn't like her, then Grady… Then Grady what? Grady wouldn't have met her if not for Taylor.

Chapter 6

Maddie took a swig of her Coke and let the fizz burn all the way down her throat. She had a small addiction to soda. Small compared to her obsession with sailing.

"So tell me about your interview." She eyed Grady. He was too cute for his own good. "How did it go?"

If she wasn't careful, she might develop an addiction to him. She wasn't sure what had driven her to bring him here, a place she went when she wanted to have some alone time. Just her, God and the lake.

He finished the Coke, a big dimpled smile filling his cheeks. She'd never been the swooning type, but she'd never met Grady.

"It went well, I think."

"That's it? That's all you're going to tell me?"

"What do you want to know?"

"I seem to remember when you were stuffing your mouth with tacos, I told you all about my father. My new father, that is." She tried to hide the hurt swelling inside, but probably failed. She had no idea what it was about Grady that had made her share all that stuff. She still hadn't been able to process through the hurt and resentment enough to share it but with only a few close friends. And she'd known Grady less than half a day when she'd told him.

He sighed a laugh. "You're right. I just didn't want to bore you with my life, but if you insist."

That dimpled smile again.

"I insist. But something about you tells me I won't be bored," she said, sending him a teasing smile of her own. Oh, what was she doing? Flirting like a maniac was not a good thing. Did Taylor have any idea of how she might react to his friend? Had that been why he'd sent Grady? He was playing the matchmaker?

"Do you want the short version or the long version?"

She laughed. "Just start from the beginning. I might as well know more about you since I'm considering staking a race on you."

And that was what she would be doing at this point. Her decision could be the deciding factor if they won or lost.

"The beginning it is." He could make her relax the way a perfect day of sailing could. "My grandfather raised me after my parents died in a car accident. I was only eight. My grandparents on Mom's side and my grandmother on Dad's side had already passed away, so it was just me and Grandpa."

Well, maybe he didn't need to go that far back. "I'm so sorry."

"Don't be. It was a long time ago. Grandpa ran a boat-repair shop up by Harris Lake and I learned everything about the business. But I went off to college like everyone

else and got my degree in technical writing from NMT—
New Mexico Tech."

She drew in a breath. "You're a writer?"

"Not exactly."

Crossing her legs, she turned to face him. "What do
you do, then? What's the interview about?"

"Patience is a virtue, ever heard that one?"

She jabbed his arm. "Go on, then."

"Before I could get a job, Grandpa died and left me
his business. It was going okay for a while but then the
lake dropped. The marinas are closed and…" He trailed
off, his gaze drifting to the edges of the lake and then the
desert horizon.

Maddie's heart went to her throat. "Grady?"

"And so is my business. I can't survive there. I put
Grandpa's business up for sale, but who would want to
buy it, things being what they are? They might want the
property for some other purpose, but not boat repair. Not
at Harris Lake."

"Oh, Grady." Maddie couldn't help herself; she slipped
her hand over his shoulder. "I'm so sorry."

He slid his gaze to her, sorrow burned there along with
something that unseated her insides.

"Here you are, trying to convince me you can race, and
you're looking for a job," she said.

When he moved to grab another soda, she let her hand
slip away.

"Yep, that's about it. Now you know everything."

Not everything. "How did you meet Taylor?"

He popped the top of the soda. "He saved my life."

Maddie leaned back. "Wow. I wasn't expecting that
one. What happened?"

He stood then. "Why don't I tell you the rest of the

story next time? It's going to get dark soon. Shouldn't we get back?"

When he offered his hand, Maddie placed hers in his, feeling the strength and assurance of his grip. She imagined someone in his line of work would have strong hands like that. "Next time, huh? What makes you think there will be a next time?" She grinned, hoping to infuse warmth in her question.

"That's a risk I'll have to take."

Heading back, the wind picked up, making the sails taut and the waters a little rough, but Grady showed himself handier than she could have hoped. He knew what he was doing, just as Taylor had said. By the time dusk had almost morphed into night, they'd moored her J24 in the slip at the pier.

Grady assisted her from the boat, and though she didn't need his help, she welcomed it just the same. "You know, Grady, I really like you."

With a smile, he shrugged and drove his gaze to the ground. Had she embarrassed him? Or maybe he didn't return the feeling. *Oh, no.*

Then his eyes were on her, illuminated by the few marina lights and the half-moon. "I like you, too, Maddie."

The way he said it, like there was something hidden behind the words, he was nothing at all like the man he'd been on her sailboat this evening, open and transparent. "I want you to be the one to race with me," she said, "but I'll warn you, the other crew members are guys and they'll likely want Sasha. She's cute and, well, need I say more?"

"Whose decision it is?"

"Let's just say I can't make it easy on you just because I like you. Understood?"

He gave her that smile she liked too much, and maybe

he knew it. "Does that mean you're giving me another chance?"

It seemed Maddie was all about second chances these days. She was giving her birth father a chance, and she'd give Grady that, too. "Just one more." She smiled. "Don't let me down."

Back at the condo, thoughts of the evening spent with Maddie swirled in Grady's head.

Don't let me down.

Just before those words, she'd favored him with a beautiful smile. That same smile he'd seen in the picture on Taylor's bookshelf.

At that moment, Grady had fought to hold himself together. Any other guy might have asked her on a real date. Leaned in for a kiss. At the very least, asked her to join him for tacos again. Something. All the vibes were there. But no, Grady Stone had to be a good guy.

Nothing wrong with that, except in the end, Grady believed that he would most definitely let her down, unless he read her wrong. Funny that not only did Taylor count on him, Maddie's words said she counted on him, as well.

He still wasn't sure where she was coming from, though. She'd taken him to the secluded cove and asked him to share his story. They had formed a connection that went beyond sailing and friendship. She had admitted she liked him, and Grady wished for all the world that Taylor didn't stand between the two of them. But Maddie didn't know about that, and Grady felt the cad for not telling her. He wasn't such a good guy after all.

But how did he bring it up? They weren't exactly crossing that lake yet.

After a quick shower and a microwave burrito, he sat in Taylor's La-Z-Boy and worked up the nerve to make the call. Worked up the strength to stay Taylor's friend. He never thought it would be so hard. Never thought a girl could stand between them. He could only hope that Taylor would treat this one right.

When Grady thought of Maddie, a fierce sense of protection rose in his chest. The problem was Grady was supposed to watch out for Taylor's interests. Keep one of the other crew members from making moves on Maddie so Taylor could pick up where he had left off when he returned. A pretty arrogant approach, if you asked him, but Grady didn't think either of them had suspected Maddie might actually take an interest in *him*. Now he wondered why not.

But he planned on getting a job and moving to California. Maybe he should emphasize that in his next conversation with her, just to be clear.

He ran a hand through his still-damp hair. Her picture stared back at him from the bookshelf.

His cell rang. Taylor.

Though dreading the call, Grady answered quickly.

"Hey, bro," Taylor said. "I couldn't get through to Maddie so thought I'd call you. How'd it go? You in?"

"Not yet."

"Why not?" For the first time, Taylor sounded worried.

"I answered a call for a preliminary interview that made me late for my first training session. But don't worry. We're going to try again. If it's any consolation, she likes me just like you said." *Oh, boy.* "All I have to do is convince her crew."

"Well, you're not going to convince them. That's what I've tried to tell you. A couple of those guys like Maddie. Why do you think I wanted you there?"

"If she's so important, why'd you have to go and break your leg?" Ouch. Grady drew in a shaky breath. "Sorry, it's just… You're asking a lot, that's all. How am I supposed to keep her from liking someone?"

Had he just given himself away?

Taylor was silent for a few seconds too long before answering. "What are you saying? Did one of the guys come on to her? Was it Ricky?"

Grady could almost hear Taylor grinding his teeth. "How would I know? I haven't met her crew yet. So if I can't convince them, then why am I here?"

Taylor huffed across the distance. "Have you not listened to anything? Maddie is the only one you need to convince. Just do what you know how to do and she won't be able to deny you."

Grady had visions of those words meaning something entirely different, of Maddie succumbing to his charm and awesome personality with an affectionate smile. A passionate kiss. He shook that image from his head. He was here for Taylor. "Okay. Just…get back as soon as you can."

"What are you not telling me?"

Why did he have to ask that?

"Hold on," Taylor said. He spoke to someone else, a female someone else. Taylor's sister? Supposedly he was staying with her in Colorado until he could get around better.

"Listen," Taylor whispered. "Shoot me an email with an answer. But right now, I can't talk about it."

A female giggle, and then after, something that sounded astonishingly like a kiss, and the call ended.

It was Grady's turn to grind his teeth.

Maddie saw Taylor's number appear on the caller ID as she talked to her birth father. She had expected her friend to call; he had started calling her every day since she'd returned from her trip.

She missed sailing with Taylor, spending time together, but she had to admit it: she also missed the *old* Taylor and their easy conversations. This new Taylor had turned positively controlling.

Regardless, she was on the phone with her father now.

Though he was her biological father—her *birth father*—calling this new man in her life "Dad" was a struggle, and she hadn't overcome that yet. Still, her heart smiled. He'd contacted her after seeing her only a few days ago.

And that brought on the question—why had he let so many years go by? He'd told her his reasons—so her life wouldn't be marred with the tug and pull between parents who had divorced. Too much to put on a child, he'd said. Instead, she had to deal with the truth of it now. When she'd learned the truth a few short years ago, her heart had ached. Admittedly, the pain grew less with each day, and with each of their conversations.

It could be worse. He might have rejected her outright. Instead, he seemed genuinely interested in spending time together. She just…she wished she could wipe the slate completely clean. Forget and forgive.

"How's your week been?" he asked. The smooth timbre of his voice sent her right back to the deck of his beautiful yacht, the cool ocean breeze wafting over her, salty waves spraying her. Maddie closed her eyes and savored the memory.

"I've had a setback on training for the regatta." She cringed at the mention of the regional J24 competition. It was nothing compared to the America's Cup, or any number of races in which her father was privileged to compete. "I know it's nothing like what you do. I'm almost embarrassed to talk about it." Why had she just said that?

"Don't be," he reassured.

Oh, how she wanted to trust that.

"So…what happened?" he asked.

"My bowman broke his leg, so now I have to decide between two other people. I think either one will work fine, frankly, but the crew and I, we worked so well together. And now I don't know."

Silence met her on the line. Was he thinking on what she'd said? Or simply had nothing to say about it? She wouldn't blame him there.

"What? No sage advice?" She regretted the words. Heard her insecurities in them.

He sighed. She wished she knew him well enough to understand what that meant coming from him.

"In fact, I have a lot to give, but was mulling over which ancient proverbs to share." He chuckled. "For one thing, be careful, Maddie. This is a much larger race than you've competed in before."

"But it's still small."

"Ah, that's what I was afraid of. Don't make the mistake of focusing on one competitor. Don't think you don't have to be strategic just because it's small. There will be a lot of boats in the water. Be cautious—sail like you're surrounded by a large fleet of competitors."

He was the more experienced sailor, of course. "Anything else?"

"Sometimes winning…" He hesitated, then, "Sometimes winning a race requires reducing speed, slowing down."

Maddie's turn to chuckle. "Right."

She'd never seen that done and hoped she didn't have to resort to that tactic.

"I'll leave you to think on that one. But mostly enjoy the race. Hang on to life loosely."

Loosely? That sounded foreign to Maddie. She held on to everything with a tight grip.

"And another idea crossed my mind…."

"Yeah?" What was he thinking now? Hearing him, Maddie almost wished she was a thousand miles away from here and back east with him, preparing to sail tomorrow morning.

"Maybe I should come down and be your bowman for this race."

Maddie tensed. That would be both the greatest thrill of her life and at the same time the greatest terror. Sailing with her infamous father—oh, but she wasn't ready for that.

He chuckled. "Now you're the one who's speechless."

"No, I… It's just…"

"I don't want to overwhelm you," he said gently. "I doubt you need me interfering at this juncture."

Was he hoping she'd invite him to watch her in the regatta? And now would be the right time for her to ask, but the idea intimidated her. Maybe he understood and that was why he wasn't pushing. At the moment, finding a full crew was enough to stress her.

"Just pray that I make the right decision," she said. *That I do my best, and that I don't let you down.*

"I will, Maddie."

She ended the call. Deep and rich, the sound of his last words echoed through her heart.

I will, Maddie. He would pray for her. Somehow she'd known he was a praying man before he'd said the words.

But there was another man in her life who was a praying man. A man whom she'd known as her father her whole life. She sighed, her heart torn. There had to be enough love and room for the both of them. Of course there was, but she never wanted to feel the way she had when she'd found out the truth—as if everything she'd believed was a complete lie. That the earth had moved beneath her feet.

And continued to shift and crush under the weight of manipulation.

She'd had no control over her life.

Maddie hated the unsettling thoughts and the negative feelings they stirred about the people she loved.

She'd give her mother and father a call tomorrow. See how things were going in Idaho. After all, Grady's parents had died when he was only eight, and Maddie would be grateful for the time she'd been given with hers.

Lying back on her pillow, she rubbed her eyes. She was the kind of person who liked to focus on one thing. Give her best. But now it seemed like she had too many things—make that men—vying for her attention. Taylor and Grady. Her two fathers.

A glance at caller ID on her cell told her just how many times Taylor had called her while she'd been talking to her father. And there was another, unexpected number.

Grady. It was after ten and she wouldn't call him back so late. Her mother had instilled that ten o'clock rule in her long ago.

She listened to Taylor's voice mails. Friendly at first. The next one frustrated. Another one—impatient. Desperate, even. Then downright demanding. The nerve. She wouldn't call him back tonight, either. Right now, she wasn't sure when she'd be ready to talk to him.

On the other hand, Grady's message washed over her like a peaceful brook. Even so, there was an edge in his tone she hadn't heard before. She thought of their time in her private cove this evening.

Her heart sighed.

God, help me make the right decision. I can't choose him just because I like him.

A lot.

Chapter 7

Friday morning, Maddie opened the store, her conversation with her father still fresh in her mind even though it had taken place two nights ago. He'd given her plenty of advice to think about. Early-morning sunlight spilled through the plate-glass window, highlighting tiny dust particles dancing in the air.

The scene reminded her of light shining in the darkness, revealing something hidden. Or something visible but unseen.

Something there all along.

Like her biological father. All these years, they could have had a relationship. Did he regret that he'd missed out on that time? Did this situation born of betrayal and deception weigh on him as it weighed on her? He'd made a life without her for more than twenty years.

She hated the downward path her thoughts had taken. Maddie wanted to grab on to the present, to the future she could have with her father, and leave the hurt and resentment behind, sunk in the past.

But that wasn't easy.

Throughout the morning, she shoved her internal struggle to the side and assisted tourists browsing nautical items, as well as locals purchasing boating gear. Maddie wished the morning would pass quickly so that Lindy would get here. She'd called Maddie earlier to let her know she wouldn't be in until after lunch.

Maddie decided she wanted to talk to Lindy about the call with her father. She wanted to talk about Grady, too, though she hadn't figured out what she would say. Lindy always listened well, and sometimes offered wisdom, but not always. Maddie didn't necessarily need advice, but someone to simply listen to her, and she loved that about Lindy. More than anything, Maddie appreciated Lindy's friendship.

As the last customer in the store exited through the front door, Lindy floated through, a smile on her face. She dangled a sparkly blue gift bag stuffed with white tissue paper. "Sorry I'm late. Thanks for holding down the fort."

"No problem. I thought you weren't going to be in until after lunch, though. I was worried that something was wrong, but I see by the look on your face that everything's right."

Lindy's smile widened. "Yes. I had a nice breakfast date with my husband."

"And the gift?"

"A little something he handed me just before I walked inside. I left him when a friend caught up to him on the sidewalk and harangued him into a conversation."

"I'm sorry."

"It's okay. We both had to work anyway, though I didn't have to worry too much. You can handle things."

Maddie smiled. "What do you think is in the bag?"

"Why don't we find out?" Lindy's eyes twinkled.

Maddie followed her into the office at the back. After Lindy tossed her purse in the corner, she yanked the tissue paper from the gift bag. She appeared as excited as Maddie was curious.

Lindy gasped. She tugged out a small black box and pressed it to her heart. Maddie couldn't remember seeing her act this emotional. She'd always seemed so seasoned with life. Tough, even. Maddie wasn't accustomed to Lindy's softer side. She acted as though she and her husband were newlyweds, but of course, Lindy's relationship with her husband wasn't Maddie's business.

Still, a morsel of envy surged inside—Maddie doubted she would ever have what Lindy had with her husband. After the lie she'd been fed, how could she trust anyone with her heart? How could she relinquish so much control over her life to another person?

The air grew stuffy. "I'm intruding." Maddie took a step back. "I'm just going to —"

"Stay with me, please." Lindy opened the box to reveal a pair of emerald-cut diamond earrings.

Now it was Maddie's turn to gasp. "Oh, see, you should have waited to open it with him."

"Then he should have given them to me earlier." Lindy fiddled with one of the earrings, working it into her left earlobe.

The door chime signaled a customer, and Maddie welcomed the escape. "I'd better get back to work. And they're really beautiful, Lindy. You're a blessed woman." To have a man like that.

And she meant that. Maddie exited the office and strode into the middle of the store, trying to shove aside that cavern of regret and loss that seemed to yawn wider at the sight of Lindy's obviously fulfilled life. Maddie searched for the customer who'd entered.

She found him.

Grady had his back to her as he studied the paintings on the wall—a lighthouse, seagulls riding the wind, a Spanish galleon in stormy waters, two racing sailboats. Her favorites on the wall were those that included Bible verses, such as the one with the clipper anchored in the quiet cove that read, "We have this hope as an anchor for the soul, firm and secure. Hebrews 6:19."

Maddie studied Grady. He had his arms crossed, his navy T-shirt stretched tight across his back and shoulders. Though cut neatly for his job interviews, his dark, coffee-colored hair would be curled and wavy if left to grow just a little longer. She'd bet he looked great in a suit.

What would it feel like to be wrapped in his arms?

Where had that come from? Her pulse shot up. She'd been standing behind him for so long, how did she suck in the kind of air she needed without drawing his attention?

But he turned to face her before she'd composed herself, as if he'd known she'd been there all along.

"Hi," she said. *Oh, please, say something else.* "What are you doing here?"

He grinned that grin she liked. Would she ever get used to it? "Maybe I'm here to buy a gift. Or to buy a picture to hang on the wall."

"Are you?"

"You like to get right to the point, don't you?" He chuckled. "I came by to see where you work. That all right with you?"

Warmth cascaded over her. More than all right. "Of course, why wouldn't it be?"

What was with this Grady guy? Even Taylor hadn't stopped by to see where she worked.

"Hey, Maddie." Lindy approached. "Who's your friend?"

Lindy had shoved her hair behind her ears to show off her earrings.

"This is Grady." Maddie gestured back to Lindy. "Grady, Lindy."

Lindy thrust her hand out. "Nice to meet you, Grady."

The way her boss and friend glanced between the two of them, Maddie knew Lindy had the wrong idea. "Grady is Taylor's friend who offered to race with me since Taylor broke his leg."

"Oh, that's right," Lindy said.

"That is, if Maddie thinks I'm up to the task." Though Grady's eyes teased her, his tone left no doubt about his confidence.

Maddie wanted to second-guess her decision to put him to the test, but this was a team effort. Either Grady could sail with the team or he couldn't.

"He looks strapping and capable to me." Lindy smiled and winked.

The woman was entirely too happy today, and although it was infectious, Maddie resisted. Maintained control.

"Why don't you take the afternoon off? You kids grab some lunch and make a day of it."

Heat breezed over Maddie's cheeks. She gave Grady an apologetic look. She didn't know what had gotten into her boss. Well, maybe she did, but she'd wanted to confide in Lindy about her father and find out what she thought. Today, that clearly wasn't happening.

"Oh, no," Maddie said. "I couldn't do that."

"Why not? I took the morning, you get the afternoon." Lindy stepped closer. "Besides, I think I'm closing up shop early."

Maddie couldn't hide her surprise.

Lindy leaned in and whispered, allowing Grady in on her secret. "Today is our twenty-eighth wedding anniversary."

"Congratulations! Well, that explains everything." Sort of.

"I'll leave you to it, then." Lindy smiled and left Maddie and Grady alone.

He jammed his hands into his jeans. "Nice."

Maddie peered through the shelves of nautical gifts on glass display cases and watched Lindy disappear. "I don't know what's gotten into her. Maybe it's like she said. It's her anniversary, but listen, you don't have to eat lunch or spend the day with me. I'm sorry if she put you on the spot."

"What are you talking about? I'd love to take you to lunch."

Take her to lunch? This almost felt like a date. In fact, their time earlier in the week at her private cove had felt like a first date, and that would make lunch with Grady today a second date. Her imagination was running wild, though. This wasn't a real date.

"Maybe you can give me a tour of the town, too," he said. "That is, unless you're the one who doesn't want to spend time with me. So now *you're* the one on the spot." He grinned that downright adorable grin.

Not fair.

Her silky ash-blond hair pulled back in a ponytail emphasized a face that looked freshly scrubbed. Her striking gray eyes peered at him, though today they appeared tired and troubled. He hoped he wasn't the reason, but no, he couldn't mean that much to her, couldn't affect her that much.

Couldn't be that important.

Not yet.

What a crazy, traitorous idea. He sucked in a breath. This wasn't about him. He was here to protect Taylor's interests. When Maddie had called him yesterday to ask if he wanted to run with her, he'd declined. Spending too much time with her could be risky and yet here he was, stalking her where she worked.

With that thought, his gut churned. Grady wasn't sure being in Crested Butte for Taylor was good for anyone, especially considering that his friend obviously had entirely too many romantic interests. With Maddie's burdened gaze, Grady's loyalties couldn't help but shift partially over to this woman. Who would protect *her* interests? Protect her from Taylor, Grady's best friend.

His chest burned caustically. How could he help them both? His reasons for being here had become convoluted.

Thank goodness the corners of her perfect lips turned upward. "I'd be happy to show you around. Let me grab my purse."

He watched her walk away, her ponytail bouncing, making her look happy and carefree, though her eyes had said something much different. Maybe today would change that. Yeah. And maybe he would stop thinking he was the answer to all her problems.

He wasn't even the answer to his own troubles.

If he wasn't careful, this little side trip to Crested Butte would be added to his list of recent failures.

While he waited for Maddie, Grady browsed the display case holding a few regional brochures meant for tourists. The idea that Maddie could give him a tour had popped into his head at the last second, but he'd wanted to persuade her to spend time with him today and Lindy had provided the perfect opening.

A citrusy scent wrapped around him, bumping up his heart rate by at least twenty knots.

"I'm ready." Maddie joined him in looking at the promotional materials.

He tugged out a pamphlet that had caught his attention and held it out. "You up for this instead?"

She pursed her lips. "I thought you wanted me to show you around town."

"A ghost town would be a lot more interesting."

Her laugh rocked him, shaking him free from where he'd anchored. He floated in her world now, further away from Taylor, further away from himself and his word and honor.

He was a traitor of the worst kind.

But when she gave him her full-on smile, he could forget everything.

"You're a funny guy. I can't make promises that a ghost town will be more exciting than a small town filled with people."

He didn't care where they went, as long as he was with her. How could Taylor have left her for one second?

Grady offered his arm and a grin of his own. "Shall we?"

Maddie slipped her hand through his arm, and his grin spread wider at the warmth from her simple touch. Maddie led him to her vehicle parked at the side of the building that housed Desert Sea Gifts. Grady opened the door for her to climb into her Subaru Outback, and she seemed taken aback.

When he was buckled into in the passenger seat, he pulled out the brochure.

"Give me that." She playfully snatched it away and spread it out across the steering wheel. "This lists about ten places, but only one is an actual ghost town."

"What do you mean?"

"A few families remain in most of these, but they oper-

ate museums, restaurants, bed-and-breakfasts, stuff to at-
tract the tourists." She pressed her index finger to a place
on the map. "We can grab something to eat here, then make
our way around the towns."

"You know, we can do something else if you prefer.
It's just that I've never seen a ghost town up close and
personal."

She eyed him, those pale grays turning silvery, and
somehow taking in more than he was ready to give. "There
are some up by where you live, aren't there?"

"Sure, but I never got around to that." Grady swung his
gaze from her intense stare to the map. "I assume you've
seen these already?"

"No." Chuckling, she tossed the brochure in his lap and
started the ignition. "Better late than never, or so I hear."

"Then how do you know so much about them?"

"I work at a tourist shop. People ask questions. I make
it my business to know."

"But you've never been there in person? Haven't you
at least been curious?"

She turned onto Main Street. "Honestly? Seeing the
ghost towns might be at the bottom of a long list of things
I'd like to experience."

Grady leaned against the seat and smiled. Now he'd get
her talking. "So tell me about that list? What's at the top?"

She headed east and out of town. "I'm not sure I know
anymore. Things have changed in the past couple of years.
In the past few weeks and days. Considering you're looking for a job in California, I'm sure you understand."

"Sure. Life can change overnight. But that's not what I
mean. I'm talking about dreams."

"Right, and those can change with life. So tell me
about your list first, then. Your dreams." Turning right,
she glanced over at him and smiled, then focused back on

the road, heading away from the lake and toward the reddish buttes in the distance.

At her question, Grady turned his head to look out his window, watching the desert flora flash by—mesquite, yucca plants and prickly pear cacti nestled in the desert grasses. A snake slithered from the road.

Sharing his dreams with Maddie Cramer—his best friend's romantic interest—had never been his intention. He'd met her on Monday, for crying out loud, and it was only Friday. But he hadn't been able to get her out of his head for one minute.

How had he gotten in this deep so fast?

Chapter 8

Grady was sailing toward the center of her heart, and if she didn't do something fast, she'd invite him inside. That could never happen. Oh, but the guy could make her wish for something more in this life. And she already wished for so much.

"My dreams. Let's see." Grady stared out the passenger window, his whimsical tone gone.

She thought back to the evening on her boat when he'd shared about his grandfather's business, and how Grady had failed where his grandfather had succeeded. She hoped her question hadn't soured his mood. "Look, Grady, if this is off-limits, maybe we should talk about something else."

He whipped around to face her, a grin edging into his lips. "You're not getting off the hook that easily."

That was more like it. She hadn't wanted to share so much of herself with anyone, but Grady made her want to open up. How did he do it?

"I'm pretty much all about sailing," she said. "So I never really thought about visiting the ghost towns. And my list isn't long."

"But you do have one, and the first five things involve sailing, I'd guess. Now that you've met your biological father, what about your list has changed?"

His question startled her. Her gaze jumped to his, and she swerved onto the shoulder before correcting. Maddie had a second to catch her breath as the junction for the ghost town appeared before them. She turned onto a bumpy, unpaved road. In the distance, she could see crumbled and decayed buildings surrounded by other structures.

"What's changed? Everything." Finding out about her birth father, meeting him, had changed her life.

"Is that a good thing or a bad thing?"

The Outback lurched and bounced, causing Maddie to tighten her grip on the steering wheel. "You don't pull any punches."

"Life's too short."

"And yet my birth father chose to waste twenty-odd years of mine."

A several-mile-long dust cloud trailed them as they pulled into the makeshift parking lot next to a centuries-old building refurbished into a restaurant. Only two other cars were there. Maybe it was too early for lunch.

Maddie shifted into park and turned off the ignition. Gazing at Grady, she rested her arm across the wheel. He frowned, but at least she didn't see pity in his eyes. No. Something dangerous to her heart stared back from behind his dusky blues.

"That's number one on your list, isn't it?"

Her breath hitched, her reply strangled.

"You want to somehow make up for that lost time." His voice was soft, gentle, understanding.

This man had gotten entirely too close, and yet hadn't she wanted to talk about this very thing today with Lindy? How did he figure it out without even hearing the details of her conversation with her father?

"Yes." The single word drifted from her strained exhale.

His smile removed the anchor from her chest, giving her back her breath. "I have a feeling you're the kind of person who, once you set your mind on something, will make it happen," he said.

Grady hopped out, leaving her staring at the empty space he left behind. Before she could think, he'd opened the door for her and offered his hand. "Come on, Maddie. I think we need to have some fun."

She placed her hand in his, allowing him to assist her out of the car. Strong and sure, his grip could almost convince her to let go of the control she so desperately wanted over her life. "At a ghost town?"

"Nothing like a good look at the dead, broken-down shell of an abandoned town to make you appreciate life." Grady squinted in the blazing sun, then slid his sunglasses over his eyes.

Too bad. She liked the intensity of his gaze.

"Why so philosophical? I thought you wanted to have some fun?"

"I do. But fun after food." His dimpled grin made her heart flip.

And his words drew a chuckle from her. "I could use some food, too."

He ushered her along the restored and creaking board-walk toward the swinging doors of the saloon, which was retrofitted as a restaurant. He held one side open for her to enter. She walked in and waited in the dimly lit room for her eyes to adjust.

"Two?"

In her peripheral vision, she caught Grady's nod to the hostess.

"Right this way." The fiftyish woman wore a dark gray pioneer dress.

Maddie and Grady followed the woman through the room scattered with tables and booths. As their shoes clunked across the newer planks, Maddie imagined a scene right out of an Old West movie, with cowboys and farmers and outlaws striding across the floor in the same way. Wild West and mining town paraphernalia littered the walls— old photographs of pioneers and locals' ancestors. Antique pistols and shotguns, mining tools, saddles. Old-fashioned utensils and dishes. Anything and everything that would have made up life for the pioneers and miners in the town more than a hundred years ago hung high for decoration, entertainment and education.

Maddie slid into one side of a booth, Grady the other. Nearby, a few other patrons were caught up in conversation over lunch. She turned her attention back to Grady. He'd figured her out much too soon. Now it was her turn, but she doubted she could read him as well. Though he seemed transparent and up front, something about him said he was complicated. Against her better judgment, she wanted to know more.

A waitress wearing britches and a gun belt strapped around her waist like an outlaw brought them ice water and menus, then left them to decide. Maddie looked at Grady until he glanced up from his menu.

"What?" he asked.

"Now it's your turn. Unless you want me to figure out your list, you'd better spill. You know about me, that sailing is my passion, and I want to recapture time with my father."

Having heard Grady say those words out loud, and now

hearing her own declaration, she realized the importance she'd placed on the regatta, the reasons for it, with clarity. How she'd tied winning the race to the hope of more time with her father, garnering more of his attention.

That overwhelmed her. That Grady had seen right through her overwhelmed her.

"Now I want to hear what's important to you," she continued, "because I know it's not sailing." Maddie studied the menu unable to meet his questioning gaze.

"And how would you know?" Grady had lived to sail, maintained his own sailboat and even owned a boat-repair business. Never mind that over the past few months the business had suffered a slow, painful death. Hadn't he shown Maddie how much he loved to sail? Why would she consider him for bowman if she hadn't seen his passion?

Stomach growling, Grady pulled his gaze from Maddie's beautiful, mesmerizing eyes and scanned the few offerings on the menu, but knew in the end he'd choose a cheeseburger. He wasn't adventurous when it came to grub. Maybe they'd ask for their food to go and find a place to eat somewhere around the collapsed structures—homes and shops from the past.

Maddie shut her menu and looked at him. "I don't know. I just think you'd find a way to stay here instead of trying to move to California." She leaned forward. "If staying close is important."

"You know, there are lakes in other parts of the country." He tossed her a wry grin and laid his menu on top of hers. "Even oceans to sail on."

But somehow he knew those were the wrong words to say, considering what she'd told him of her father. Did she wish she was back east sailing with him?

When the waitress approached with her pen and pad,

Grady read her name tag. "Sharon, can we get our food to go?"

He eyed Maddie and saw her surprise, her eyes brimming with approval.

The waitress lifted a brow. "Depends on what you plan to order."

"A cheeseburger's portable food, right?" Grady glanced at Maddie.

"I'll have the same," she said.

"I don't have cups you can take with you for drinks," Sharon said, "but you can grab canned sodas from the museum across the street."

"That sounds perfect." Grady handed her their menus.

While they waited on their burgers, Maddie used her forefinger to circle a knot in the varnished pine table. "The way you talked about your grandfather and his business... your business, if sailing was important to you, you'd figure out how to make it work. That's all I'm saying." She lowered her head. "It's really not my place."

No, it wasn't. Though her words stoked his inner struggles, he couldn't help but wonder—did she care if he left or stayed in New Mexico? That couldn't be it, and yet the conviction behind her comment left him with that very impression.

He leaned against the seat back and drummed his fingers on the table. "That would be my dream—for my business to succeed." To be something other than a failure. His intention had been to get her talking about herself, not to divulge so much of his personal struggles. "But let's say all that was in place, that I had a thriving boat-repair business, could go sailing any time I wanted, I'd like to do some traveling around the country. Maybe even Europe. Scotland and Italy would be nice."

Best to get them to a safer conversation. Bringing up

the dream list wasn't supposed to have taken such a serious turn.

She smiled, something in her eyes letting him know she also preferred a lighter conversation. "Scotland. I'd like to go to Scotland, too. Definitely Italy. Alaska someday, too. You?"

Before he could answer, she frowned. "Excuse me."

Tugging her cell from her tan-colored jeans, she stared down, then smiled. "I need to take this call."

"Okay."

"You can say hi, too."

Huh?

"Taylor, hey," she said into the cell as she watched Grady.

Oh, no. He almost shook his head, hoping she'd understand he needed to hide they were having lunch together. But why should he hide that? Because he wasn't there as Taylor's friend, that was why. He was there with her due to his own interests. He stared at the table she'd found so interesting moments before, unable to meet her gaze. Watch her expression as she and Taylor talked.

Their waitress returned with a big brown paper sack. "Your cheeseburgers are inside along with crispy fries. Eat it while it's hot."

"Thanks," he said.

Maddie continued her conversation with Taylor, her head tilted away from Grady and the waitress.

When the waitress left the bill, she turned away, but Grady stopped her. He pulled cash from his pocket and slid it across the table. "Keep the change," he said.

She winked and left. Once she'd gone, Maddie turned back to Grady, her cell still at her ear. Grady rummaged through the sack to find their lunch.

"Sitting across from Grady. He's a good guy. Thanks

for sending him to help." Maddie's voice sounded sweet.
Playful.

He glanced up to catch her watching him, a question in
her eyes. He smiled to chase it away. He hoped she hadn't
noticed his obvious discomfort at listening in on her conversation. He didn't need her asking him about it.

"He's sitting right here, you want to tell him yourself?"
Nausea roiled.

"Okay, sure, I'll tell him." Maddie laughed.

Grady blew out a slow, even breath, hoping Maddie
wouldn't notice that, either. She laughed again, apparently
caught up in her banter with his best friend.

"How's the leg?" She lowered her eyes, and Grady felt
like she had forgotten he existed.

As she chatted with Taylor, Grady noticed how her eyes
sparkled, which made him think that maybe he'd been
wrong about Maddie and Taylor's relationship. Maybe she
was into Taylor and Grady was trying to steal her away.

Sliding from the booth, he went in search of the rest-
room to splash his face with cold water. Inside his chest,
his hero grandfather's words—about being a trustworthy
man that others could count on—ricocheted.

Chapter 9

Armed with a couple of sodas from the vending machine and their sack lunch, Maddie and Grady strolled the streets of the ghost town—if one could really call it that, since not everyone had left the place, preferring to stay behind and use their skills to showcase the town to travelers. She and Grady found a quiet spot on a pile of crumbled stones next to what used to be a barber shop, if the fading sign was correct.

They ate quietly at first, and then shared stories from their childhood. After hearing a few tales about a young Grady, first with his parents and then with his grandfather, Maddie wasn't so sure that sailing wasn't as important to him as it was to her. But perhaps for different reasons. Different but the same—it was all about memories or making them.

When they finished eating, they found a trash receptacle for their garbage. Maddie led the way across the street to the Miner's Store and Museum, happy to see that the lunch crowd had grown. Sad enough to witness a ghost town, but even more depressing when the restaurant and museum didn't draw at least a modicum of interest from tourists.

The sun baked the desert, leaving dry, dusty air, heightening the whole ghost-town experience. Next to the museum stood the rock wall of a building, and that was it. Nothing but the one wall.

Other structures near the museum had also yielded to the crush of time, leaving behind two or three deteriorated stone walls. In the distance, a continual dust cloud plumed from the main highway, suggesting this particular ghost town was among the most popular.

Grady strolled beside her. "I wonder what this town would look like if the silver hadn't died out."

"What would the whole state look like, for that matter?" she asked. "If all these towns were thriving instead?"

Maddie was glad that Grady had finally loosened up. He'd seemed distant for a while after Taylor had called. Or maybe it had started before that, when he'd been talking about his dreams. Warm, friendly and open, he was exactly the kind of person she felt comfortable confiding in, but she sensed he held something back. She didn't know him well enough and couldn't blame him for having secrets. She had her own.

But when it came to Grady, she was more than curious; she wanted to know him better.

Once again, he opened the door for her. A real gentleman. Maddie hadn't been around enough of them in her life. She had assumed that sort of old-fashioned courtesy had gone the way of medieval knights.

"Thanks," she said and entered the museum.

Musty oldness wafted over her, overpowering the fresh scent of Grady's aftershave. That was probably a good thing. "Oh, I almost forgot." She turned to Grady. "Taylor said he'd call you tonight."

Grady snorted.

"What?"

"There's no surprise there. He calls every night."

"You, too, huh?" she said. "I guess he just feels left out since he's stuck in Colorado with a broken leg, that's all. He probably feels lonely." Now maybe she could find out why Grady had acted strange when Taylor called. Maybe they'd gotten into an argument.

Grady shrugged. "Yeah, lonely."

"Why do I get the feeling you're being sarcastic?"

He flashed his heavyweight grin. Did he know how disarming that was?

"I don't know. Why do you?"

"Well, I'm glad I answered. I was supposed to call him back and never did. I was frustrated with him, but not anymore." He'd eased back into the old Taylor whom she knew and trusted.

"Oh, yeah? Why?"

"Well, he's your friend, too, and I probably shouldn't say anything, but he's a little controlling in my opinion."

"And you don't like to be controlled."

"No, actually, I don't." Or manipulated. Maybe that was part of why she enjoyed sailing so much—to harness the wind and have power over it gave her a sense of control like nothing else.

Before she could stop Grady, he paid the small fee for the both of them to enter the museum. "I hope that wasn't too controlling for you," he said.

"You don't have to pay for me, too. This isn't a date or anything." Maddie watched his reaction, and almost wished she hadn't said the words. Saying them brought an unbidden disappointment.

"We're using your vehicle. Your gas." The grin slid from his face. "It's the least I can do."

He led the way into the museum where they perused tools and equipment needed to prospect and mine silver ore. An old-fashioned stove, dishes, pots and pans, kitchen tools and clothing of the day, and even a shrine to one of the town's pioneer women were on display.

Grady stared at the vintage dental tools spread on a table and pointed at pliers. "You think you could do it?"

"What? Pull a tooth or let someone extract one from me?"

"Either way."

She chewed on her lip. "I think I would pass out."

"Me, too." He chuckled. "Visiting the dentist is my least favorite thing."

But then his smile revealed good, strong and straight teeth. "You obviously don't miss your appointments," she said.

"My father was a dentist. And my grandfather took pretty good care of me, too. What I can say? I'm grateful for him, but I would have given anything if my parents hadn't died in that accident."

"I'm glad that you had your grandfather." *So sorry about your parents.* She had more than her fair share.

The pain etched in his face was too much. She turned her attention back to the antiques and artifacts as they strolled through the ghost-town museum, wishing they could get back to happier conversation.

Grady drew in a weighted breath. "I can't imagine how it must have felt, learning that the man you thought was your father wasn't your father after all. That there was… someone else."

He had no idea. "I'm working through it, trying to put it behind me and focus on my father, the one I just met."

Her heart was still tender and raw to the touch for the love she had for both the fathers in her life.

"That's good. You have a lot to be thankful for."

She nodded her agreement, and they finished the tour of the museum. The rest of the day, they kept their conversation to light and fun topics as they visited two more ghost towns. Finally, she parked her Outback by Desert Sea Gifts and next to Grady's two-door Mazda.

He didn't open his door to escape her vehicle, but instead faced her. "I had fun today, Maddie."

She liked the way he said her name. Even during the more uncomfortable parts of their conversations, Maddie was glad she had been with Grady.

"I did, too." She expected a response. A smile. Something. Instead, he just stared.

What did she see behind his eyes? Regret? Longing? He seemed torn, but whatever it was, Maddie couldn't breathe under the crush of it and glanced down.

What was happening between them? She hadn't known him long. Didn't know him well. Today had seemed like a date, a second date, if you counted their evening in her cove. She hadn't meant for that to be a date or the time she spent with him to turn into something other than getting to know a guy she would sail with in the regatta. But they had a connection she couldn't explain.

"Grady...I want you to be the one to take Taylor's place. For a whole lot of reasons that have nothing to do with sailing." There. She'd said it.

He laughed. She could so get used to that.

Gathering her courage, she forced her gaze up to meet his. Did she imagine it or had he inched a little closer, disturbing her in a million different ways? Her heartbeat pounded her awareness. "I wish I hadn't told Sasha I'd take her out for a test sail. We have to choose the best one, and I have to be fair to my crew, too. Not just pick you because I like you."

"I think you said that before." He lifted his hand and played with a strand of her hair, making her breath come too fast. She had to control it, to steady the rise and fall of her chest.

"Plus, I'm betting you really want to win," he added. "So you have to choose the better sailor."

Slow your breathing. Don't let him see how he affects you. "That's true, too." With Grady this close, she'd almost forgotten how important the race was to her. Unfortunately, that could be a detriment to everyone involved.

"Next week, we'll meet at the dock and you'll sail with us. I'll…we'll…make the decision then."

Grady cupped her cheeks with both hands. Maddie closed her eyes as if it was the most natural thing in the world. As if she knew what was coming next. She could hope. And why she wanted this man to kiss her she couldn't fathom. All she knew was that it felt right.

She sensed his nearness, and knew he would kiss her. She *wanted* him to kiss her. Crazy. Her emotions filled her sails, sending her off course and too fast. Her attraction for him went deep, much deeper than anything physical. It was inexplicable.

"I'll have to be tough on you," she whispered. "Throw everything at you, so they won't know."

"Know what? That you—" His lips met hers.

Strong lips, they pressed against hers, softly at first. Then he drew her closer, nestled his hands behind her head, weaving his fingers through her hair. Her mind and heart floated some place she'd never been. Never known existed. Some place spiritual and physical at the same time.

But she hung on, kept control. Though everything inside wanted to let go and float to this foreign land that was

Grady, she anchored herself—she didn't know where—but she couldn't drift without direction.

Without being the one at the helm.

Maddie's soft lips were supple, and…responsive. Making him lose his mind. Why, oh, why was he kissing her? What were they doing?

But with his lips joined with sweet Maddie's, his hands tangled in her luscious mane, Grady could almost forget his priorities. What was most important. Because Maddie had taken over an island in his heart.

Too fast, this was much too fast. Never mind this shouldn't happen at all.

Even though he could almost forget, he hadn't completely lost his head. An image of Taylor flitting across his brain wouldn't let him. Grady was here for his friend, watching over his interests because Taylor trusted Grady to be dependable. Trustworthy.

Even if Taylor's demands were misplaced, even if Grady's loyalties were torn between Taylor and Maddie now, this wasn't right. The ugly truth washed over him like a squall and, edging back, he disengaged.

Maybe he should back out of everything. Go to California before this whole thing blew up in his and Taylor's faces, leaving Maddie hurt.

Guilt ridden, he drew in a painful breath, preparing to apologize for the forbidden kiss. But then he'd have to tell her everything. Taylor's trust would be blown, as well as Maddie's. Besides, Grady was too much of a coward.

She spoke first, though. "I know it seems crazy that this race could mean so much to me." Her silver eyes shimmered and held him captive. Pled understanding and warmed his heart. "I know I haven't exactly made things easy on you, but I'm glad Taylor sent you to help. I understand that being here is a sacrifice, considering you need to find a job."

Sacrifice, right.

Kissing her was everything he could have wanted in a kiss. Everything he shouldn't. How could he back out? Maddie needed him too much, even if he still had to prove himself to her and her crew.

He brushed her silky cheek with his thumb. Maybe he could salvage this gently. "The race is important because it's in your blood and, having met your father, now you know why. Now you have even more to prove." He let his hand drop away and looked down to break their emotional connection, hoping it would work. "And I probably shouldn't have kissed you."

With her slight intake of breath, he added, "I don't want to distract you. We both need to focus on sailing. On winning." There, he'd been as gentle as he could. Did even that small concession hurt her as much as it hurt him?

Should he just back out now before it was too late?

When he dared to look up, appreciation flooded her gaze.

Grady, you're in trouble.

He kicked the door to Taylor's condo shut behind him and slumped in the La-Z-Boy, scraping both hands through his hair.

I shouldn't have kissed her.

Leaning back and pressing deeper into the chair, he sighed. *Shouldn't have kissed her.*

He'd stated as much in a feeble attempt to stop the momentum. Instead of slowing things down before it was too late, keeping the regatta a priority had endeared him to her even more. Or so it seemed. If only she knew.

Grady was more traitorous than a double agent. If he

stepped away from this predicament, he'd let both Taylor and Maddie down. But he'd also let them down if he endured to the end.

The only move left to Grady, really, was to lose the right to race. As it was, he couldn't see this ending well. At least moving on sooner rather than later would save them all a lot of heartache. Except the race was important to Maddie, and Grady wanted to make sure her dreams would come true. But she had Sasha—who was Grady to think she wasn't a better sailor? He presumed too much.

On the side table, his cell vibrated. Dread crawled over him as he saw Taylor's face on the smartphone. Grady shouldn't have kissed her. How many times would he chide himself? Talking to Taylor right now would be a disaster.

He let the call go to voice mail.

Chapter 10

Sitting on the *Crescent Moon* as it rocked gently in her slip, Maddie tilted her face to the sun and let the warmth soak in. It was a perfect day for sailing.

She hoped Grady would show up.

The breeze kicked up about ten knots along with her pulse. She hadn't heard from him in a week. Not since their kiss. But he'd been right to say he shouldn't have kissed her. From the beginning, she'd suspected he would be a distraction. And now more so than ever.

Add to that, there wasn't much space she could put between them on her keelboat. Race with him, and she could very well lose her concentration. The way she felt when she was with him almost made her care about something other than winning. Almost. That alone was bad news. If there was one thing she'd learned in her sailing experiences, it was that she needed to maintain control over herself, the boat and her crew, and when it came to winning, control and command were more important than tactics.

Losing focus because she liked Grady wouldn't do her crew any good. But she didn't have a choice now.

Sasha's test run had been a disaster. Even the crew of the *Crescent Moon*—Cameron, Lance and Ricky—who'd much prefer another female on their team, could not ignore that Sasha's rhythm had been completely off. She wasn't accustomed to the kind of weight distribution needed with the five-person crew on a J24. Maddie or one of the others had to continually tell her when to shift positions to fore and aft, or side to side, or to keep out of the way. Something Taylor had instinctively known because he'd sailed with them long enough. At one point, Maddie thought they'd actually capsize, and then, worst of all, during a jibing maneuver, Sasha had failed to move quickly enough as the boom swept 180 degrees across the boat, knocking the poor woman overboard.

A shudder ran over Maddie at the memory.

Sasha had quit right there in the water.

Grady was Maddie's only hope now. She was out of time and options.

Closing her eyes, she enjoyed the feel of the sun's heat prickling across her skin. She thought back to the moment she'd tried to forget all week long, the moment when they'd shared a kiss. He'd pulled her to him and pressed his lips against hers—and with the thought of their nearness, her pulse soared on a fifteen-foot wave.

She swallowed. Now wasn't the time to think about that.

But considering they hadn't spoken since then, she wasn't sure he would even show. She'd left him a message and he hadn't confirmed. He didn't seem like the kind of guy to back out without any word.

Boards creaked behind her, informing her that someone approached. Her heart jumped. *Grady...*

She opened her eyes.

Clark Nielsen.

He strode toward her wearing his typical white pants and navy commodore jacket and matching cap—his attempt to look official.

"Maddie," he said. "Haven't seen you out training with your crew in a while. I guess your new crew member didn't work out?"

Why did he want to know? "Everything is fine. Thanks for asking." Maddie ignored his condescending gaze. When it came to sailing, Nielsen was ruthless.

"So where's Natasha?" she asked. "You two are still together, right?" Oh, she did not just ask that. Didn't need him thinking she had an interest in him. Never had and never would.

Why couldn't he just leave?

His grin spread wider. Maddie wasn't anything like Natasha, the type of woman he obviously preferred. So why did he always give her the feeling he was in pursuit?

"Mind if I join you?" He gestured to her boat.

Oh, she minded, all right. "Not at all." But what could she say without being rude?

Looking for her crew, who'd gone to grab some drinks, Maddie glanced behind Nielsen as he stepped from the pier onto the *Crescent Moon*. And where was Grady? Her day was sinking along with her heart.

Nielsen propped himself next to her. "I'd offer my services, help you crew the *Crescent Moon* for the regatta if I wasn't racing myself."

Maddie wished she could genuinely thank him for his offer. But she'd known him too long and too well. She hadn't forgotten the collision and his attempt to intimidate her out of his path.

"Oh, you just want the chance to be on the winning team, that's all." She gave him her own challenging grin.

"We'll see who has the winning team." His smile couldn't hide the hint of menace in his tone.

This race was important to him, too, and for far different reasons. Maddie could almost wish she hadn't met her father. Not yet. The pressure built behind her temples.

More creaking boards behind her. Maddie twisted around.

Grady... Her heart leaped. She wasn't sure if it was because his appearance would send Nielsen away or something more, but she had a feeling it was the latter.

"There he is," she called out, sounding too eager. Let Nielsen think what he would.

Even though he shot her the grin she adored, his eyes swam with concern. He remained on the pier and Maddie hopped from the *Crescent Moon* to join him, followed by Nielsen. Grady thrust his hand out. "Nielsen, right?"

"That's correct. And you're Grady."

Grady nodded. Maddie could tell something bothered him. Was it Nielsen?

"I was just informing Maddie that you'd better be good. There's a lot of competition for the regatta."

Grady's deepening frown set Maddie on edge. What was that about?

"I wouldn't be surprised if we didn't see some of the competitors show up a week or two ahead of the regatta to get used to the local conditions," Nielsen said. "Fine-tune their boats. This class has the most restrictions, you know?"

"We'll be ready for them, you can count on that," Maddie said.

Nielsen tipped his cap. "See you later."

Good riddance.

Maddie wasn't sure what she'd expected when she saw Grady for the first time since their kiss. A hug? Another kiss, maybe? Not really. But she certainly hadn't expected his downcast demeanor.

"What's the matter, Grady?"

His eyes flashed. "Nothing. Why do you ask?"

She didn't have time to play games. Spotting the other three crew members finally leaving the marina shop—they must have seen Grady—she waved them to hurry.

"Listen, Grady," she said, "I'm counting on you today."

"How'd it go with Sasha?" he asked, though he barely sounded like he cared.

"Not so well. Okay? It's you or nothing. Do you understand?" *Please, let him be everything I need him to be today.* "These guys? There's nothing to keep them sailing with me. They could join another crew, or make their own way." True enough. Even though they'd practiced and trained for a long time, losing a crew member changed everything.

And Grady—she didn't want to need him so much. Needing someone meant losing a measure of control. But this race was a team effort. Too bad she had the feeling her need for him had nothing to do with this race and more to do with her heart.

Grady edged away from her—putting an imaginary line between them?—and glanced over his shoulder.

"Will you please say something?" Tension hedged her tone. Was he bailing on her? And she'd let him kiss her! This race and her heart—her life—seemed to teeter on a ledge, waiting for Grady's reply to push her over.

Maddie held her breath and eyed him. His gaze melted with warmth, though unease still etched his brow. "You'll get everything I have, Maddie, don't worry. I'll do my best."

More silver than gray glinted in her eyes as she squinted up at him in the sunlight, a gentle breeze tossing strands of hair against her cheeks. Soft cheeks, as he recalled. He'd meant to wipe that memory from his thoughts, but here it surfaced again at the wrong moment.

All he wanted to do was pull her slender form into his arms. Kiss her again. With the imminent approach of her other crew members, he pulled himself from her gaze and took in the sleek little J24 keel, preparing himself to give his best when they sailed on the *Crescent Moon*. Give his all to Maddie Cramer and this regatta.

He'd come here today with every intention of letting Sasha be the better sailor. She might have been without any help from him. Not giving his all when Taylor counted on him to watch over Maddie—protect her from the wolves who might date her and take her away—had scratched against the grain of Grady's belief system. But Taylor's request had grown all manner of thorns Grady couldn't begin to navigate between.

Standing on the pier with Maddie, invisible barbs bristled around him. She didn't know about the barbs. He wished he didn't know about them, either.

"Hey, guys," she said, smiling at them. "I'd like you to meet my friend Grady."

My friend, not Taylor's friend.

"He'll be our bowman." Maddie turned to face him. "Grady, this is Lance, our trimmer, Ricky, the driver and Cameron, our mast man. I'm the tactician and your skipper, of course." She grinned, completely in her element. "But you already knew that."

Grady shared handshakes with Lance, Cameron and Ricky. Ricky was the one Taylor mentioned might be interested in Maddie. Lance was a tall, lanky, geeky-looking guy. Probably owned a computer-repair business. Cameron didn't look old enough to have his driver's license, though he had to be in his twenties, and Ricky, with his thick neck and shoulders, was definitely a jock. Had probably played football in high school.

"You're Taylor's friend," Lance said. "I heard about his big rescue."

What grand story had Taylor told them? Reminding himself that sailing with these guys meant he needed to win them over, needed them to like him, he relaxed and smiled. "Yeah, I'm forever in his debt."

"You haven't paid him back? I can't imagine that guy hasn't gotten into trouble that didn't require you to bail him out in some way." Ricky laughed, and the rest joined him.

Grady laughed a little, too, while Maddie watched.

"We're in some trouble now, man." Lance thrust his hands into his khaki cargo shorts. "We need to train for this regatta, be prepared. All of us thought we had a serious shot at heading to nationals."

"Until Taylor had to ruin it for us." Cameron hopped onto the *Crescent Moon*. "Now we're hoping you can save us. Or at least help us compete."

"Winning would still be good," Lance said.

"Maybe this will repay Taylor." Ricky chuckled.

Yeah, but not in the way Taylor hoped. Grady's gaze jumped to Maddie. He hated that none of them had a clue about why Taylor had sent Grady. Did it even matter why, really, if they needed someone to sail them to the nationals? "I'll do my best to be your man."

"Make that bowman," Cameron said and fiddled with the mast, readying the mainsail. Lance and Ricky climbed aboard, too.

Ricky glanced back at Maddie. "You coming, Skipper?"

Maddie nodded at Ricky then touched Grady's arm— that one act sending him back to the forbidden moment. "Are you ready?" she asked.

Had their kiss affected her so monumentally? His only

hope was that it had meant nothing to her, except the gleam in her gaze said otherwise. His insides contracted.

"Sure," he said, and stepped aboard.

All these big guys on this little boat. And with Maddie. No wonder Taylor wasn't comfortable. If Grady was interested in Maddie, he might be protective, too. Jealous, even. Unfortunately, that same emotion snaked through him when Maddie fell into Ricky, who gently assisted her.

Yeah, he understood now. He was no different than Ricky. No better than Taylor. Grady wasn't trustworthy or loyal or anything special. He was just another guy who liked Maddie.

She didn't waste any time on small talk, and the next thing Grady knew they were on the lake, following the shoreline in an effort to simulate the actual regatta.

Grady had to admit a thrill rushed through him at the chance of being part of this crew. Their enthusiasm impressed him, stirred him to meet the challenge. To be honest, he wasn't sure how he was going to perform to his own standards, much less Maddie's. But getting into position at the foredeck—a place he was very familiar with thanks to the few races he'd competed in before the water level had dropped at Harris Lake—felt like second nature. As bowman, all he had to do was focus on the halyards and everything forward of the mast. He made sure the jib tacked right, let the trimmer know about trim, let Maddie know about other sailboats and lake traffic, set the spinnaker pole and hoisted or doused the foresails per Maddie's call. Whatever was needed. He didn't think about anything else, just allowed everything to flow from his hands instinctively.

His grandfather always told him he was a natural. Maybe it was as simple as that.

Maddie could have put him at the mast and had him

focus on pulling the twings and staying out of the way,
but she'd trusted him with Taylor's old position, and that,
mostly at Taylor's suggestion. She trusted Taylor, and
Grady hadn't wanted to let either of them down in the
smallest of ways. He breathed easier knowing that he
could follow through. At least in this one thing he could
be counted upon.

The rest—he wasn't so sure.

A half hour in, the crew's rhythm was syncing as if
Grady had always been part of their team. Grady was in.
Would have been in, regardless of how Sasha had performed. As the wind powered the sails and drove the boat
around the lake, for a moment Grady's gaze drifted out
over the water and to the lakeshore.

He hadn't sailed in much too long, and yet it all seemed
to come back to him, as if it was meant to be. He was meant
to be here on this boat with Maddie.

From his forward position, he glanced back at her where
she stood in the pit and caught her watching him. She
smiled, her eyes warm and pleased. Grady hoped the others
didn't sense the current between them. He hadn't wanted
this to happen with her. Hadn't expected it.

But he wasn't sure how to stop it. Maybe if he showed
up for sailing practice and kept his distance otherwise,
he could make it through the race without getting closer.
Without another kiss. After all, he'd made it through a
whole week without talking to Maddie after the kiss. What
kind of guy does that? But she understood why—getting
involved in the middle of this race wouldn't do them any
good. He hadn't thought she'd be so easily convinced—
but this regatta was important to her because of her newfound relationship with her father. She wanted to impress
him and Grady understood that.

He thought he would go crazy not calling her, not stopping by her store or her apartment. Thank goodness he'd told her early on he couldn't run with her. He knew he had to be strong—stronger than he had been. Once they established their training schedule, he'd see her more, but somehow he had to stop these out-of-control emotions.

For Maddie.

For Taylor.

There was no doubt he was drawn to her for more reasons than he could count, and for plenty that he couldn't even name, but he didn't deserve her. She was passionate, driven and destined to win. Grady felt like he was floating without direction.

But if anyone didn't deserve Maddie's heart, it was Grady's best friend, Taylor.

Chapter 11

The next week cruised by much too fast. After a long training day on Saturday, Maddie and the crew met at Perry's Pizza Parlor, the tantalizing aroma of garlic, spices and cheese teasing her nose, making her mouth water. She sat crunched between Ricky and Lance in the corner booth, with Cameron on the other side of Lance. Grady faced Maddie from across the corner booth. She hadn't wanted to sit right next to him, thinking that would be safer, but now she sat across from him and she couldn't get away from his midnight-blue eyes.

She couldn't afford to let Grady distract her. She had to keep her focus on training for the regatta, maintaining her self-control, her command of the situation and her crew. When it came to Grady, her thoughts were frazzled. She almost wished she were positioned at the *Crescent Moon*'s bow so Grady would be behind her, and she wouldn't have to constantly watch his trim, athletic form in action, which only made her think about his arms around her. And that kiss. Followed by that thoughtful apology that showed he understood she didn't need a romantic distraction. He realized how important the regatta was to her.

Maddie fought the dreamy sigh that almost escaped her lips.

If the guys were to sense that she had a thing for Grady, it could throw this perfect synergy they'd obtained way off course. But sitting across from him, looking into those lake-water eyes, might just be worse.

Plus, she needed time to figure out exactly what it was that drew her to him. She didn't know him that well. But how long did it take? She'd had a lifetime with her parents, and that hadn't prepared her for their big reveal. Maddie shoved those thoughts far away. Tonight she wanted to enjoy a camaraderie she hadn't experienced in a long time. Even with Taylor around, there'd been some tension between him and the rest, but not with Grady.

They'd ordered two large pizzas—one pepperoni and one supreme. Tunes from the seventies and eighties played on the old jukebox in the far corner, and the lights were low for the Saturday-evening crowd. Maddie stretched, searching for a little elbow room between Ricky and Lance. Feeling more content than she had in a long time, she released a small sigh.

They'd sailed four times this week, training for the regatta, which was only three weeks out. Grady was a natural. He was amazing. Why hadn't she trusted Taylor about him from the beginning? Really, her stubbornness had been about Taylor, not about Grady's abilities. Her need to control the situation could have cost them Grady.

She watched him caught up in a conversation with Cameron about boat repair. She heard more about epoxy, fiberglass and boat motors than she ever wanted to hear.

Those two had a lot in common and, from the sounds of it, knew their stuff. Grady got along with everyone—he was one smooth sailor. But the old cliché made her wonder if there wasn't something wrong just under the surface to mess with her world. She should know to search for the secret—everyone had one.

The waitress brought their drinks and interrupted the boat-repair discussion.

Maddie took a sip of her iced tea, hoping to get in a word, but Lance beat her to it.

"So what's next, Grady? Where will you go after the race?"

The pizza arrived and interrupted Grady's response. Maddie knew he was job searching, but other than sailing together, they'd kept their distance. No morning jogs. No long telephone conversations like Taylor tried for every evening. And for some reason, Grady's answer might just matter to her more than it should.

They'd shared a kiss. One kiss. That didn't have to mean anything, did it? Funny that one kiss had changed everything. With a slice of pizza on her plate, she waited for it to cool and for Grady's answer. He took a bite, as did the others, and Maddie watched them gobble up their slices like nothing else existed. Maybe Grady had forgotten the question. They had all worked hard this afternoon and were hungry men after all.

Next to her, Ricky guzzled his soda, finishing it off. "I'd like to hear the answer to Lance's question, too, Grady. I mean, we all have a vested interested in knowing. What if we actually won, then what? We'd want you to race in the nationals with us."

Grady wiped his mouth with his napkin. "Taylor should be back by then."

"I think I speak for all of us when I say you're a better fit," Cameron said.

Maddie almost spewed her tea. The guys stared at her, laughing and joking.

Ricky rubbed her back. "You okay there, Mads?"

She couldn't believe Cameron had voiced that without some sort of private discussion first. What about Taylor?

Grady eyed her over the rim of his glass. "I'm not sure you're speaking for Maddie."

Wow. All four sets of eyes on her, Maddie fought for composure.

Lance rocked his glass back and forth, the ice clinking. "I think all Cameron means is that if you help us win this, you need to be the one who sails with us in the nationals."

"And I think you guys are getting way ahead of yourselves," Maddie said, finally getting a word in. "We have to win this regatta first."

They couldn't just push Taylor out. But a small piece of her heart would love to keep Grady sailing with them for much longer.

"Isn't that the point? And if we do, Grady is the better sailor. Guys, I just said out loud what we all are thinking." Cameron took another slice of pizza from the pan and stuffed half of it in his mouth.

Good. She didn't want to hear more. Maddie toyed with her crust, her heart sinking for Taylor. She looked up to catch Grady studying her. Probably reading into her expression all the wrong things.

"And that brings me back to my initial question," Lance said. "Where will you go after this race? Are you going to stick around? Because even if we don't win this one, there will be others."

The waitress appeared and refilled their glasses.

Grady repositioned himself in his seat, obviously considering his next words while he waited for her to finish. Then he said, "I appreciate your vote of confidence, guys. It's been a pleasure sailing with you, but I can't step in to take Taylor's place if he wants it back. He's my friend. I'm only here to help. As far as me sticking around, I need employment, and I'm looking for a high-tech job in California." He glanced across at Maddie. Gauging her reaction? "I can't say what the future will bring. We'll have to see how things play out."

Her heart kicked a little—she'd probably read more into his words than he'd meant. Since keeping their distance, it seemed she'd turned to second-guessing everything. Was he doing the same?

"Well, I need to hit it, guys." Lance pushed his plate away. "I'm worn out, and I've missed church the past two Sundays. I don't intend to make tomorrow three."

"You're such a backslider," Cameron elbowed him.

Lance looked at Grady. "You found a church yet?"

Grady stared into his tea. "Actually, I've been driving back home to Harris to attend my church."

"They go to Grace Fellowship," Ricky said. "I go to Community Church with my grandmother."

"When you go, that is," Cameron said. To Grady, he said, "Consider yourself invited."

Grady grinned. "Thanks. I'll think about it. Might be nice to visit somewhere local."

Taylor would visit church with her sometimes, but Maddie never saw him as that committed, spiritually speaking. Where did Grady stand with God? For that matter, she should never have let him in so far without knowing. But he was leaving, he'd made that clear. None of it mattered. They hadn't known each other that long, so why was she even thinking in terms of something more with him?

"Maddie?" Ricky said her name.

She realized the boys were staring. "What did I miss?"

"When are we meeting again to train? With the regatta only three weekends out, do we need to bump up the schedule?"

"I need to look at my calendar. I'll let you know tomorrow." What she really wanted was to talk to her father about how hard to train and when to rest. At some level, she had enough experience to know, but she'd never competed in a regatta of this magnitude.

There was so much at stake.

Winning.

Impressing her newfound father.

And she had to admit to one more thing—keeping Grady with her longer.

Somewhere after the first bite of pizza, Grady had lost his appetite, but now as he unlocked his car, his stomach grumbled. He turned at the sound of footfalls behind him.

"Hey, Maddie," he said. He opened the door and peered at her from the other side.

Taylor's phone calls had slowed; he'd likely call Grady tonight and ask about their sailing day. Grady didn't want Maddie's face lingering in his thoughts or heart while he talked to his friend. Hard enough as it was, without her standing in front of him, her dusky eyes staring up at him, looking wounded for some reason.

Grady glanced to the shopping center across the road, keeping the door between them.

"I'm sorry if the guys put too much pressure on you," she said. "I didn't know they felt that way. I hope it wasn't too awkward."

"I'm glad that I can sail with your crew. But I won't lie, the conversation did feel awkward. Taylor's my friend.

I'm not here to take over his position." Grady swiped his hand down his face.

He wasn't here to steal Taylor's girl, either—his imagined relationship with her anyway—or his position. Right. Man, this was getting convoluted. He'd never thought being a friend could be so difficult.

"The guys didn't mean anything by that. It's just that sometimes you have to make the hard decisions. Maybe… maybe it's time for a new crew…that's all." Maddie's voice dropped. "Mix things up a little."

"I don't know that I feel the same way. Could be there's something wrong with me. Maybe it's because my grandpa drilled into me that loyalty, that my word and honor are important."

Maddie stepped around the door and reached for his arm, found purchase and squeezed. "And those things are important to me, too."

"Yeah, well, that's all I have right now. Lost my business and I don't have a job." He'd said too much, had revealed his insecurities.

Maddie released his arm. "You're a good friend, Grady. You don't have to worry about that. I hope you know that you have more than great character going for you."

"Yeah, sure." Another stack of rejection letters and emails kept him from believing it.

"Taylor knew what he was doing when he sent you. He knows you're better at sailing than he is. He told me that much." Her lips edged into that smile Grady liked.

He'd bet Maddie's cute grin had been the first thing that had attracted Taylor, too.

When would the guy come back and take up where he left off? Let Grady get on with his own life?

"Are you okay?" Maddie's brows furrowed.

"I'm fine. Don't worry about me." Her concern dissolved his frustration for the moment. He wished he'd met her under different circumstances. It would be nice to talk to Taylor about this girl he was crazy for.

Yes. There it was. He was crazy about her. But he couldn't be.

"See you at church tomorrow, then?" she asked.

"Sure, why not." Save him the drive home.

Home? Where was that anymore?

The next morning before church, Grady found himself at the Crested Butte Diner sitting across from Bob Lawrence—one of the old Vietnam veterans his grandfather had served with. Grady had received the call last night after watching Maddie exit the pizza-place parking lot. He could hardly believe the guy was here in the flesh. Bob had convinced Grady to meet him for coffee before church, assuring him he didn't mind the drive down from Harris.

Bob wore a fishing shirt and a Red Sox baseball cap, his silver hair splaying from the sides. "I was sorry to hear about your grandfather. Real sorry. I thought I'd make it out to see Henry at least one last time."

Grady took a sip of his coffee and studied the guy. "I'm sorry I had to be the one to break the news."

Bob had stopped by the boat-repair garage expecting to find a thriving business and his longtime friend, Henry Kirk, but instead he'd found the place listed for sale. He'd called the number Grady had left with the Realtor and that was when Grady had told him the news about Henry's passing. Of course, Grady had bought Bob breakfast—the least he could do, considering the guy had driven down to see him.

"Thanks for meeting me," Bob said. "I heard from your grandfather on occasion, and he always spoke highly of you." He winked, then worked on his bacon and eggs. "Said you were going to take over the business one day."

He glanced up from his food, squinting one eye at Grady.

At Bob's comment, Grady's breakfast soured in his stomach, though he didn't believe the man had meant any harm, but rather had meant his statement as a compliment. "I'm afraid I haven't done him proud on that one."

"What? Because you're selling? You can't blame yourself for that. If the lake is low and business is down, nothing much you can do about it."

Grady bit off a piece of crunchy maple bacon. "So tell me your side of the story."

"My side?"

"Grandpa always told me how important a man's word was. Said that people's lives depended on it. He never went into much detail, because he wasn't the kind of man to brag about his accomplishments. He was a hero, I know. I want to hear more. I could tell he wanted me to understand."

"And do you?"

"I think so. He drilled it into me enough. That if I don't have honor and integrity, don't keep my word and I'm not loyal, that I'm not worth much." And Grady was feeling pretty worthless lately.

The man across from him chuckled. He finished off his breakfast and appeared to contemplate the rest of the story. Finally, he pushed his plate forward a bit and nursed his coffee. "You want my side of the story? Then I'll give it to you."

Their waitress, a cute brunette, stopped at their table. "Need a refill?"

Bob nodded. "Thank you."

Grady shook his head. "No, thanks. Maybe later."

When she was out of earshot, Bob continued, "I would

have followed Sergeant Kirk, your grandfather, anywhere. Done anything for him. He was that kind of man. I remember it like it was yesterday. It was the morning of September 23. We were involved in an aggressive assault against the enemy. But the Vietcong gave as good as they got, and they turned it around on us. The next thing we knew, we were hiding in the thick forest and under heavy fire." His eyes took on an eerie look, as if he was reliving a vivid memory. He shook his head a little. "I can still hear the rockets and the machine-gun fire. Feel the heat prickling over every inch of my body in the hot jungle."

His focus came back to Grady. "That's when Sarge stood up to the enemy and crossed the shallow river and captured the bunker where the enemy had taken cover. We all followed, except for the two of us who were wounded. Me and Arnie. Your grandpa came back and got Arnie. I don't know how he did it, automatic weapons going off, bullets whizzing by all around us. But he promised he would return for me. I'd never known him to go back on his word, but I didn't want a promise from him. I told him to leave me. Not to risk his life. I was done for anyway."

Itching to hear more, Grady urged Bob to continue. He was running out of time if he wanted to make church. Would Maddie be disappointed if he didn't show?

The veteran drank his coffee, then locked eyes with Grady. "I can't tell you how hard I held on to the feeble hope that your grandfather would do exactly what he had said. I didn't want him to, but the part of me that wanted to live prayed he would return. I survived on the hope of that promise, and let me tell you, he was a sight for sore eyes when he came back, but then he had taken a bullet, too. Still, he helped me. I was in bad shape. In the end, our company went on to win the battle. So that's my story. I'd still do anything for him today, if he were here."

This guy owed Grady's grandfather for saving his life, and he would have done anything for him in return. Just like Grady owed Taylor for saving his. Grady's chest squeezed.

The vinyl booth creaked when he moved. "I'm glad I got to meet you. I just wish Grandpa was here, too."

How would his life be different if Henry Kirk was still alive? For that matter, if his parents hadn't died in the accident. Would Grandpa have kept the business going? Or would he have closed it, too? Regardless, Grady missed his grandfather. His words of wisdom and encouragement. Some days he struggled to remember that his grandfather wasn't there anymore. Maybe he'd taken him for granted, thinking that he would always be there for him.

"So what's *your* story, son?" Bob lifted his cup to his lips.

His question surprised Grady, though he wasn't sure why. "I need a job. Direction." *I need a life.* "In the meantime, I'm here helping a friend out by sailing in an upcoming regatta. And…I'm struggling to keep a favor I promised."

Might as well lay that much out there and see what Bob had to say.

"Your grandpa kept his word to me that day. I don't think I would be here if he hadn't come back and saved my life. But I didn't ask him to make that promise. I wouldn't have blamed him if he hadn't returned. Anything could have kept him from fulfilling his words. It was a war zone after all." He studied Grady.

Was he waiting for Grady to say more? He hadn't wanted to promise Taylor anything, but he owed the guy. Just like this man had owed his grandfather.

"So did my grandfather ever call in the favor?"

"No."

"Do you think he would have at some point, if he were still alive?"

The man shook his head. "Not a chance. I would have done anything for him, but he wasn't the kind of man to ask."

Chapter 12

Maddie strolled toward the front doors of the church, her short conversation last night with her newfound father still playing through her mind.

"You're doing all the right things, Maddie," he had said. "I can't wait to see you race in the regatta."

"What?" she had asked.

"You heard me right. I'm coming down to watch. I wouldn't miss it for the world. That is…if you're okay with that."

"Oh, yes. I want you there." She did, didn't she? It terrified her, but at the same time it meant the world to her that she mattered to him.

She wanted to believe that she had *always* mattered to him. That he'd simply lived up to an agreement that he'd made with her mother and adoptive father years ago. An agreement they had thought best for Maddie. But if she thought about the situation too much, she experienced that little pang through her heart again—somehow she had to move past it.

"It's settled, then," he had said. "I'll email you my itinerary once I've made the arrangements."

Then she'd told him she'd pick him up from the airport.

Maddie's focus came back to church when one of the deacons smiled and opened the door for her. She stepped inside to hear the contemporary worship band practicing for the praise and worship service. She hoped her father would stay long enough to attend with her.

As she moved down the aisle of pews, she thought about how meeting her father had changed her life. A small part of her hoped that he would invite her to join him in Stamford, Connecticut, so she could sail on the vast ocean waters with him, and often. However, she'd never been a city girl, and wasn't sure she was made for anything but her little lake on the desert.

Stepping into the pew where she usually sat, Maddie reined in her wishful thinking. Putting too many hopes on something could leave her shattered and disappointed. She never knew what lurked in the shadows. Her love for the father she'd missed all these years was genuine enough, but she could never trust anyone completely, including him.

Grady caught her gaze as he stepped into the same pew as her. He'd worn a suit, and the sight of him did funny things to her insides. She hadn't been the same since he had walked into her life, had walked out on the pier and waited for her that day. What was it about him?

He was yet another person she'd grown more than fond of, but he, especially, posed the risk of throwing her life out of control. Seeing the question in his eyes, she offered a small, shaky smile, and gestured for him to join her. Lance and Cameron sat with their friends and family. Maddie had sat with her mother and adoptive father—would she ever get accustomed to thinking of him this way?—until they'd moved to Idaho.

The music hadn't ramped up yet, and people still stood around chatting and finding their places. Grady sidled up to her. "You look nice," he said.

Maddie glanced down at her yellow dress accented with purple flowers. "This old thing?" She glanced back up. "Oh, that's right, you haven't seen me in anything remotely girlie."

She saw the admiration in Grady's eyes.... Oh, she had not just said that. Heat swarmed her insides all the way up her neck.

Best to move his attention away from her. She took in the crisp white shirt, tie and suit jacket. Probably his interview suit. "You look nice, too."

"Yeah, I think I'm overdressed," he said.

"We're pretty casual around here, although some guys wear business attire."

Pastor Will spoke from the pulpit, bringing the gathering to attention. He opened with prayer and then the music grew louder. As Grady sang "Open the Eyes of My Heart, Lord" next to her, Maddie noticed he had a nice voice. That he knew all the words and didn't stumble through the song delighted her. But she needed to focus on worshipping God herself, and quit thinking about the guy who stood mere inches away. The guy whose words from last night echoed through her thoughts.

I can't say what the future will bring. We'll have to see how things play out.

For some reason, she'd taken that to heart as though he'd been talking specifically to her and *about* her—about them. But that was crazy, wishful thinking on a hope and a dream she didn't have a chance at. How many times did she have to remind herself? He'd made it clear enough last night that he wasn't staying.

When Taylor came back, Grady would leave. Or if he got the job he wanted, he would leave sooner. Even if he stayed, or at least saw them through wherever this regatta would take them, hadn't Maddie hoped her father would invite her to stay with him in Connecticut anyway?

She longed to get to know him better, to make up for lost time. And to sail on his magnificent sailing yacht. She dreamed about sailing with him in one of the more prestigious races, but she doubted that would ever happen. Still, it would be enough to watch from the sidelines. Cheer him on, knowing that he'd take her out again on the water. He hadn't remarried after the divorce, but Maddie had to consider he might have a romantic interest in his life who might not appreciate Maddie moving in or living somewhere close.

Regardless, getting too attached to Grady could derail her dreams of getting to know her father better. Trusting Grady with her heart might leave her devastated.

Maddie quieted her chaotic thoughts, turning her heart back to God. She knew she had issues; she needed to forgive her parents and somehow trust them again.

For the first time in her life, she felt as if she steered out of control and without a rudder, when control was the very thing she wanted the most. But even if she were in control—*really* in control of her own life—too many desires fought to win her over. Confusion reigned.

The song ended and Pastor Will took the pulpit. The congregation sat down and Maddie refocused her attention to listen to the sermon.

The pastor cleared his throat. "God wants control of your life. He wants to be Savior *and* Lord."

* * *

Grady was glad that he'd attended Grace Fellowship this morning. The music was awesome and the sermon was powerful. Plus, he'd experienced all of that while sitting next to the beautiful Maddie Cramer in her pastel yellow dress with the lavender flowers that made her look soft and dainty.

This was a side to her that he'd had yet to see. After all the sailing they'd done together, he should have at least glimpsed this softer side to her. As it was, he'd only suspected it. He knew her lips were soft enough—and with the unbidden thought, his insides stoked. He shouldn't be thinking about her lips—about that kiss—while sitting in church, though the service was almost over.

As the pastor finished, Maddie hung her head. Grady glanced her way and spotted the lone tear sliding down her cheek. Concern for her wrapped around him. What did he really know about her? In fact, what was going on in her life right now outside of sailing? He knew a little about her birth father—had something happened to upset her? Or were the tears for something much deeper? Something spiritual that Grady had no business concerning himself with?

But he wanted to do something. Clutch her arm like she'd done last night when she'd tried to reassure him of his worth? She wiped at the tear and dropped her hand in her lap to rest on her burgundy leather Bible.

Grady didn't know what else to do, but he couldn't stop himself. He had to do something. He slid his hand over the top of hers and squeezed. She opened her hand and let him in.

He sat next to Maddie and they held hands. They'd already shared a kiss, so why did holding her hand seem out-of-bounds? He and Maddie had sailed together well, danced around the kiss and their attraction, both knowing that in order to concentrate on the regatta, they shouldn't get involved. Both knowing that their lives had met at this point, but from here went in very different directions.

And Grady had one more thing than she did to keep them apart—his best friend, Taylor, wanted Maddie for himself. But with Maddie gripping his hand in her soft palm, Grady couldn't take his hand back. He'd never felt this sort of peace and contentment before, just sitting next to her in front of God and everybody.

When Pastor Will asked that the congregation bow their heads for prayer, Grady obliged. He had a prayer of his own.

Oh, God, please show me what to do. Help me be a man of my word. Be a hero like my grandfather—a grandson he could have been proud of. Help me do the right thing by Taylor. Help me do right by Maddie. I don't want to love her, but I think I'm falling for her. How could she love me back if she ever found out the truth? How could I live with myself?

Help...

With the prayer over and the service dismissed, Maddie released his hand. He could only hope that she would release his heart, too. Did she have any idea how he felt about her?

On Wednesday, Grady slept in because he'd stayed up until the early morning hours submitting résumés and looking for potential employers online. It was beginning to be a bad habit.

With the pillow over his head, he almost didn't hear the "I'm Alive" Peter Furler ringtone.

He grabbed his cell.

Dynamics Corp?

His pulse thundered. They were calling him back? He'd already had a phone interview with them. He sat up and took all of five seconds to compose himself in order to sound professional. This could be it—a real chance at a great technical-writing job. Maybe he wouldn't have to feel like a failure anymore.

Grady answered the call with enthusiasm, pleased that he didn't sound as if he'd just woken up. Job hunting was an all-encompassing job in itself.

"Grady Stone speaking."

"Hello again, Grady. This is Jim with Dynamics. We'd like to fly you out for an interview, that is, if you're still available."

Grady's spirits soared for the rest of the call as he worked with Jim to coordinate a flight out to California tomorrow. Tomorrow! When the call was over, Grady entered the details into his computer calendar and smartphone. Then it hit him.

Tomorrow he was supposed to sail with Maddie and crew. They'd sailed on Monday and Tuesday and obligations kept them from sailing today. But tomorrow they were back at it, except now Grady couldn't make it.

His spirits took a big dive into the shallow end of the lake. He'd need to let her know, and he hoped they could reschedule for Friday. He'd held her hand three days ago, and now he felt like a real louse with no honorable intentions toward her. He'd figure out how to share the news with her—though now he wasn't sure if it was good or bad news. He had to wonder: if Taylor didn't stand between Grady and Maddie, would Grady be working to stay in Crested Butte instead of trying to leave? But the truth was, he couldn't hope to support himself, much less a wife and family, without a job. He couldn't have a family, be a father and even a grandfather one day, until he was no longer a failure. Until he found something at which he could succeed.

Wife and family?

*Whoa...whoa...*where had that come from? Grady ran his hands over his face, sifting through the mad rush of thoughts, Maddie at the heart of the images flashing in his mind.

He would call Taylor to let him know the good news about the interview, and count on Taylor's voice to be a cold splash of reality.

His best friend answered on the first ring. "Hey, bro. How's it going?"

"I have an interview in California tomorrow, thought I'd let you know."

"That's great news. I knew you'd land a job. And the timing couldn't be better. You'll have time to race before they want you there for work."

"It's not exactly a job offer yet, but I feel really good about it, you know?"

"Yes, I do. Had that feeling a few times myself."

"How's the leg?"

"Fair to partly cloudy. Thanks for asking."

"When are you coming back to your pretend home in New Mexico?"

"I'll be there for the race. That's going okay, I gather. Maddie thinks highly of you."

"Yeah, we sail well together. Glad I could do this for you."

Grady squeezed his eyes shut, uncertain about his next words. "So you're coming back in a couple of weeks. What about your girlfriend there?"

No taking the words back now. But he had to know. Maybe throwing it out there like that would catch Taylor off guard and he'd answer without thinking. Not that he needed to hide anything from Grady, but considering the favor he'd asked, stringing another girlfriend along was pretty low.

"Oh, she has to work. It's not like she can take that many days off." Taylor made a funny sound. "Listen, Grady, Maddie is still the girl for me, okay? If that's what you're worried about, just don't. It's not like I'm cheating. We aren't even together."

Grady ground his molars for a few seconds before replying. He couldn't exactly wish that Taylor hadn't saved him that day, but he could wish that someone else had. "Since I'm doing you this big favor already, I'm going to do you another one. Tell you the truth. Maddie isn't interested in you. She…she met someone else. I couldn't stop that from happening. Don't know what you were thinking by asking this favor, but as far as Maddie goes, you're wasting your time."

This wasn't even about Grady's interest in her. He'd said those words hoping that Taylor would let go and move on, because whether or not Grady was in the picture, Taylor was bad news for Maddie.

And as much as he hated to think it, Taylor was bad news for Grady.

Chapter 13

At Desert Sea Gifts, Maddie flipped the closed sign over on the front door.

"You've been down all day, Maddie. What's up?" Lindy sipped on her straw, sucking the last of her drink, then set the empty can down. She walked over to a closet and pulled out the vacuum cleaner.

Maddie moved to the cash register to close it out. "I'm a little frustrated, that's all. Grady wasn't available to train today. That's why I switched my afternoon off to tomorrow. He had a job interview in California." Disappointment had taken hold last night when Grady had called to inform her of his interview.

At first, she'd been ecstatic at his call, thrilled at the sound of his voice. Grady had gotten under her skin and there was no going back. But then he'd shared the news. Sure, she'd been happy for him—and she was, really— but that meant they couldn't train today. What if something happened and he had to leave the racing team for the job when they were already so close to the regatta? She couldn't replace him. Not in two and a half weeks.

But it was more than that. Just the thought of him moving away to California when she was only just getting to know him left her deflated. Would there ever be someone she could count on?

Lindy peered at her from across the store. "I'm about to start the vacuum. You want to talk about it or not?"

Maddie waved her hand. "I'll be fine. I'm just getting nervous about the race, that's all."

Lindy started across the store toward her. Maddie thought she knew all Lindy's looks. The motherly advice look, the what-for look, the get-out-there-and-show-them-what-you've-got look. But this one… Maddie had no idea.

When she reached the counter, Lindy drew in a breath. "I've put this off for too long, Maddie. But I need to tell you something."

This couldn't be good.

"I've stood on the sidelines and watched people jerking your chain for too long. Your family, and now your new friends. I hate seeing your life being pulled this way and that way because of other people's plans. And now—" Lindy's voice cracked "—I'm going to do the same thing."

Maddie's knees trembled. "What are you talking about?"

Lindy straightened and dragged in another long breath. "This is all good. It's all good—I have only one regret."

Would the woman please tell her what was going on?

"I'm selling the store."

Maddie's jaw dropped.

Lindy rushed on. "Mitch wants to move us back east close to where I grew up. A few weeks ago, we were thumbing through some old photo albums and I guess that reminded him of our visits there. He'd love to get into sailing something bigger, plus he gets along great with my family. It's always been his job or his folks keeping us away from the coast. But now his parents have agreed to come, too, once we get the logistics worked out."

Lindy bubbled with more excitement than Maddie had ever seen.

This was good and right. For Lindy.

Maddie swallowed. "I don't know what to say."

"Oh, Maddie." Lindy came around the counter and gave her a long hug. "You have been the best employee and friend. You've been like a daughter to me, so that's why I haven't known how or when to tell you the news. That's my one regret—that I'll be leaving you."

Coming to work every day to see Lindy for the past several years, listening to her advice—Lindy was the only solid and stable thing in Maddie's life. Until now.

The store, her livelihood.

Maddie pressed her palms to her cheeks. "I'm so… happy for you. When…when are you—"

Lindy grabbed Maddie's hands and pulled them from her face. "It'll take a while, so please don't worry. Whoever buys this place, I'll make sure they know you are the best employee they'll ever find. You know your way around. Your job is secure here. I'm listing the store next week, and we're selling our house and looking for another out east. Again, it could take months. But I needed to tell you."

Maddie stepped back and leaned against the wall. So many changes happening too fast.

"Maddie." The way Lindy said her name, Maddie knew she was about to offer advice. But she wasn't sure she wanted to hear any.

Another person to pull everything out from under her. But she should have known better than to count on even the smallest of things like a job. Her friend Lindy always

being there for her. Look what happened to Grady. He'd
lost a business. A person couldn't count on anything or
anyone to keep them anchored.

Except me...

The still-small voice dropped into her heart, but she
didn't want to hear even that.

"Listen to me, Maddie." Lindy peered at her. "This
could be your chance to do something with your life. Get
out of this small desert town. Have you thought about
going to stay with your father? You really should consider
asking him about that. He owes you some of his time."

Maddie could only shake her head.

"I've said too much, I'm sure." Lindy winked, an attempt to infuse levity as always. "I know you like the new
guy, too, and that's why you're down today. He's gone
off pursuing his life and dreams. He knows he can't find
those here."

Except what if Maddie was part of his dreams? With
Lindy's words, Maddie realized that she'd held on to that
hope and how wrong she'd been to do so.

"Look at you. You're crying. Oh, hon..." Lindy pulled
Maddie to her shoulder. "I'm so sorry if I hurt you. That's
the last thing I ever wanted. But you don't let that boy hurt
you either, okay?"

Maddie let the tears flow—this might be the last chance
she'd ever have to just...let go. Lose control. Remembering how a tear had slid down her cheek during the church
service on Sunday appalled her—worse that she suspected
Grady had been watching.

When the tears were spent, she pulled away. "I'm sorry
I got your blouse wet."

"It'll come out in the wash." Lindy tugged a tissue from
the counter and handed it over. Maddie blew her nose and
smiled at the funny look on Lindy's face.

"About Grady," Lindy said. "I know I said don't let him hurt you, but I think he just might be one of the good ones."

Maddie laughed into the tissue as she blew her nose again. Everyone liked Grady, including her. Lindy's news about selling her shop and moving away had sent Maddie tumbling, but she appreciated the truth. The sooner she knew, the better prepared she would be to find her way when someone else ran the shop. When Lindy was gone.

"Thanks for telling me, Lindy. I understand how hard that was."

Pain etched the older woman's features. "I know what you've been through and I should have told you as soon as I knew, but I didn't know how."

"No, I get that." And maybe she understood a little better about her parents. Once the truth was hidden, it was so much harder to reveal it as the years passed.

Maddie sniffled, feeling better for letting go of all the pent-up emotions, if only for a few minutes.

"Get out of here, kid. I'll finish closing up." Lindy flipped on the vacuum cleaner, apparently done with the conversation.

Just as well—Maddie had a lot of thinking to do.

She went home and changed, then headed to the lake, grateful that she could sail alone this evening to nurse her wounds. Lindy leaving. Grady in California on an interview. Leaving eventually, too. What next?

After parking her car, Maddie made her way to the marina and then started for the pier where her boat waited. She noticed Nielsen preparing to take his brand-spanking-new J24 out—for some reason, he'd recently secured the slip next to the *Crescent Moon*.

Maddie wasn't in the mood for even a simple hello, so she skirted the dock and strolled away from the boats toward the lakeshore until she found where the brown sand met the water. How long had it been since she'd walked the shore? In the distance the sun moved toward the horizon, though it wouldn't set for at least three more hours.

Clouds gathered near the buttes in the distance, and a breeze kicked up a few knots, cooling the moisture that had already started gathering on her back. In the shadow of a bluff overlooking the lake, she spotted someone else walking the shore.

The familiar form and cadence squeezed the breath from her.

Grady.

Wearing flip-flops, Grady kicked up sand on the beach. He was enjoying the peace and quiet of the desert lake—so unlike his experience in Ventura, a city filled with noise, people and smog. And the traffic! If he got the job, he'd have to live close to work. After growing up in Harris, New Mexico, he'd probably go crazy if he had to drive that route every day. Though his aunt lived pretty far from Dynamics, he might have to stay with her for a few days or weeks until he secured the right place to live. But maybe he was thinking too far ahead.

Today, he'd caught an early flight and after one connecting flight, arrived by eleven-thirty. Had an interview lunch, met a few people and then flown back. He'd stopped off at the condo to change out of the monkey suit and then decided on walking the lakeshore to think. Pray.

The interview had gone better than he could have hoped. *Thank You, God.* He'd given his all, and the personalities clicked. All the ingredients for a great future were there.

All except one.

Maddie.

It was almost as if he could have one but not the other. In what future could he have both Maddie, whose life was here, *and* a technical-writing job in California? In what future could he be with Maddie and have a clear conscience because he'd been true to his word? Been loyal to his friend?

Despite all his doubts, he wouldn't rule out a relationship with Maddie just yet. A life with her might be possible. With God, all things were possible. Grady believed it; he just wanted to see it. He stopped and faced the lake, admiring the calm water, a few sailboats in the distance.

Maybe he should bring the *Habanero* over to sail. Why hadn't he considered that before? But then he might hear something soon on the job. The regatta was just barely over two weeks away, and then what? The crew talked about winning, but what if they lost? What reason did he have to stay on when Taylor returned to take back his position on Maddie's crew?

To try to claim her for himself—when she wasn't his to begin with. Nor was she Grady's. Or anyone's. She wasn't a possession. His last conversation with Taylor hadn't ended so well. Grady's words about Maddie had gone unanswered when Taylor's Colorado girlfriend had interrupted the call and Taylor had hung up.

What a mess.

"Hey." The familiar voice drew his attention and sent his heart skipping.

"Maddie?" Seeing her brought a grin to his face. "What are you doing here?"

Her blond hair hung over one shoulder as she made her way toward him, leaving footprints in the sand. "I could ask you the same thing."

He chuckled. "Yeah, well, I caught an earlier flight

back, actually. I didn't know how long the interview would go. I guess we could have sailed this evening, but I didn't want to mess your schedule up again."

"I figured it was something like that." She smiled softly.

Looking over the water, she stood next to him. He thought back to when he'd held her hand in church, and wanted with everything in him to reach for her now.

"I know I don't see you every day as it is…" Was he really going to say this? "But I missed you today."

Her laugh made his insides dance.

"What do you mean? You could see me anytime you want."

"That's just it. When I was in Ventura today, I couldn't see you." Grady stared out over the lake, unwilling to risk a glance at her face.

But the next thing he knew, her soft hand gripped his. She'd been the one to reach for him, and he smiled down to his toes.

"Want to go for a walk?" she asked.

"Where?"

"Away from the marina would be nice."

"What? No sailing for Maddie Cramer tonight?"

She squeezed his hand. "I came out here to think."

"Me, too," he said, and they walked along the shore toward the bluff, the sun casting long shadows now.

With her hand in his, it was hard to care about anything else—but then, to have the life he wanted, he'd need a way to provide. He reminded himself he was going much too fast with all this, and he didn't want to scare Maddie away. He'd have to work things out with Taylor first, if he even could. But he reminded himself that God was the God of the impossible.

All good intentions, but would they be enough?

As they continued walking and holding hands, a current of mutual affection linked them together.

"So how did your interview go?"

"The interview went as well as it could. But I'm not the only one they're interviewing. The process of the actual hiring can take a while, though." He was glad for that. Maybe he'd have time to figure out what he had with Maddie, if anything. "You said you came out here to think. What about?"

She huffed. "Life is funny sometimes. You have a great opportunity for a future in technical writing, and I just learned today that Lindy is selling Desert Sea. She's moving away."

Grady stopped and turned to face Maddie. "What?"

Her striking eyes blinked slowly up to meet his. "She assures me the new owner will keep me on, but really, how can she make that promise? I just… It made me realize how much I counted on her and the store always being there. How stupid I've been. How I've put entirely too much focus on sailing my little boat in a small lake."

When she shook her head and turned from him, releasing his hand, Grady drew her back. He pulled her into his arms, and she came without hesitation. He held her, pressing her against him, hoping to infuse her with reassurance. But what did he have to offer?

"I'm sorry, Maddie."

She released a tiny shudder. Had she been crying? She tugged free and smiled. "You know what? I changed my mind. I want to go sailing after all. With you, Grady. Just you."

The way she looked up at him at that moment, she might set his dreams on fire. She was so beautiful.

Grady ran his thumb over her silky cheek. He wanted to kiss her. Oh, he wanted to kiss her.

But he resisted.

Chapter 14

Maddie couldn't think of any place she'd rather be than at her private little cove—with Grady. Maybe with all the changes in her life, and especially after what Lindy had told her, she was emotionally vulnerable. She didn't care, though. Maybe that made her too needy, but with her life slipping out of control, she needed the cove.

She needed Grady. From the first moment she'd met him, she knew there was something different about him. She couldn't explain it, or put her finger on it, but it could be as simple as the fact that he listened. Really listened.

She sat on the edge of the boat and let her feet dangle. Grady had removed his lifejacket to get comfortable and lay on his back, staring up at the sky as the sun settled in the horizon. They'd have to leave much too soon, but even a few moments here brought her peace.

With his hands clasped behind his head, he glanced at her with a contented expression—that everything was well with the world. The guy didn't even have a job, so how did he manage that kind of peace? But maybe he was about to get one and he knew it. Sensed it somewhere deep inside.

Maddie sighed. The job would take him from her. She'd never planned to let him in like this, to trust anyone ever again.

"What's wrong?" His simple question—showing that he cared, that he wanted to know and listen—somehow soothed the tension building at the back of her neck. Stiffness that had brewed over the past and the future. Over her inability to trust.

"Nothing." Everything. This thing with Grady—whatever was happening between them—she hadn't planned on it, and it was happening at the absolute worst time and place. They were two sailboats crossing paths, heading in different directions.

If nothing else, they had this moment in time. Something inside her must have known he would be special to her, because she'd brought him to this place the first time they'd sailed. She thought back to their conversation then.

"I was just thinking that last time we were here, you never finished your story. You said it was getting dark and we needed to head back." She brought her legs up and rested her chin on her knees.

"Which story?"

"About how you met Taylor. You said he saved you. What happened?"

"Are you sure he never told you? The rest of the guys made it sound like he told a pretty grand tale."

"He never mentioned it. No."

"It's getting late and we need to get back." Grady's face lit up with that grin that made her heart sing.

"You." She shoved him, but not too hard or he would have fallen right into the lake. Hey, now, there was an idea.

"We'll head back after you tell me."

Grady's smile fell.

Why didn't he want to tell her? "Is it upsetting to remember? I'm sorry if I'm being too intrusive."

"No, it's okay."

He glanced up again, eyes as dark as the lake. He couldn't know how much she wanted to run her fingers through his hair. She wished they were that close, but... not yet. In one swift move, he sat upright and hung his legs over the side.

Somehow in changing his position, he'd ended up close to Maddie. Really close. Their legs were practically touching. Grady hung his head, making her even more curious about his story.

"You okay?" she asked.

"Yeah. Trying to think where to start."

"How about the beginning?" She'd said similar words to him the last time they'd been here. Then he'd told her his story, at least some of it.

When he angled his head and smiled, her insides shook. Did he feel that, too? He tore his gaze from her and looked out over the lake, a few whitecaps here and there as the breeze swept over the water. "I'd gone to visit a buddy from school in Colorado. We went mountain biking."

Maddie gasped, thinking of Taylor and his broken leg. "What is it with you boys and mountain biking?"

Grady nodded. "Pretty weird, huh?"

"So, what? Did you fall off your bike? Did Taylor pick you up and dust off your knees? How did he save you?" She cringed inside. Hadn't meant to make little of it.

"Something like that, only much worse. I tumbled over a cliff. Hit my head and fell in a river."

At his words, she stopped breathing, she was sure. Sitting taller, she tensed, waiting to hear the rest.

When he didn't continue, she squeezed his arm. "Grady? What happened next? Please tell me. I can't believe you didn't die from the fall alone."

"Taylor was down by the riverbank. He pulled me out and did CPR. That's all there is to tell. He saved my life. We've been friends ever since."

"That's some kind of friendship. You must be very grateful to him."

"You have no idea."

The way he said it... Maddie let that sink in. "What do you mean?"

"I think I'd like to go for a swim." Grady stood and pulled off his shirt. "How about you?"

Maddie got up, too. "You're not getting off that easy, Grady Stone. What did you mean by that?"

Grady stepped off the boat and plunked into the water, splashing Maddie. She screamed and laughed. She had a swimsuit in the cabin down below, just in case, but she didn't usually like to swim.

When Grady's head came out of the water, his wet hair was slicked against his head, appearing almost black. "Come in with me. The water's perfect."

"Perfect, says you. It's not usually warm enough for me." Maddie shook her head. "No, I'm into sailing, not swimming."

"Suit yourself," he said, and floated on his back, looking happy.

Why'd he have to go and ruin their moment? For that matter, why'd she have to ask him about Taylor? Everything was nice until she'd asked him to tell her the story. The mood had shifted after that. She recalled the day at the restaurant in the ghost town when Taylor had called. Grady's demeanor had changed then, too.

Grady splashed her, getting her attention. "Earth to Maddie. You looked a million miles away."

"Not so far."

"I need a hand getting back on the boat," he said.

"Sure you do."

He thrust his hand up. "No, really, Maddie, just help me get back on the boat."

"You don't need my help. You're going to pull me in."

"No, I'm not."

"Give me your word."

"I never give my word lightly." Grady made to get back on the boat, and Maddie offered her hand.

When he took it, he fell backward, bringing Maddie with him, and the tepid water swallowed her whole. She came up spewing and spitting mad. Maddie punched him—a friendly punch—but she wanted him to know she wasn't happy.

"Why'd you do that? You gave me your word."

"No, I didn't. I said I don't give my word lightly."

"Oh, you. Now look at me. I have a swimsuit in the cabin. I could have changed." She swam for the boat.

Treading water, Grady caught her and turned her to face him. "I'm sorry. I thought you'd laugh. Thought we'd have fun, that's all. Forgive me?"

How could she stay mad? "Of course I forgive you. I guess I'm just not any fun."

"That couldn't be further from the truth." He drew her near, and cupped her cheek with one hand.

She could barely breathe as goose bumps broke out on her skin. "Grady, I…"

He kissed her then, the way she'd wanted ever since that first time. Drew her to him and made her feel like she was the only thing that mattered to him. Heat roared inside her head, rushed to her heart, swirled through her insides.

His tenderness made her long to trust him completely. *God, please let him be real.*

Chapter 15

Kissing Maddie's sweet lips, with the water lapping around them in her peaceful cove, Grady didn't want to let go.

He was betraying Taylor, but everything about kissing Maddie felt right. From the moment the mainsail had caught wind and powered them forward, he'd been thinking about how to get her in the water. Thinking about how to kiss her.

His lips curved into a grin and he broke away—ridiculous!—but he pressed his forehead against hers, not wanting to lose their connection. Not so easy as they bobbed in the water.

"What's so funny?" she asked.

"You should have seen the look on your face when you realized you were right—that I was going to pull you into the water."

Splashing him, she giggled and edged away. He let go and she held on to the boat. "What?"

Her wet hair dripped around her face and shoulders, accentuating the natural look that he'd loved since the first time he had seen her. "You're beautiful, you know that?"

Her cheeks turned pink. "Thank you. You're not so bad yourself."

Grady searched her eyes for any sign of regret. He didn't see it. This time he wouldn't tell her they shouldn't have kissed, that it would only distract them from the race. They were already in deep, no matter how much they ignored it.

She glanced at the sky, the colors deepening as evening progressed. "We should get back."

Reluctantly, Grady climbed onto the boat and reached for Maddie, helping her up.

"I'll grab a couple of extra jackets I keep down below," she said, and disappeared.

The breeze picked up and carried the promise of a cool evening, sending a chill over Grady. He rubbed his arms and considered his predicament, if you could call it that. Maybe he'd given too much weight to Taylor's request. When his friend had admitted to having a girlfriend in Colorado, Grady had been furious. Kissing Maddie hadn't exactly been payback, but he'd stopped denying the obvious—there was something deep and strong between himself and Maddie.

He didn't think he could ignore it any longer, but everything in him told him to be a stand-up guy. A man of his word. Yeah, right. Before this whole thing went any further, the best thing he could do was be completely up front with Maddie—tell her why Taylor had asked him to help her—the whole story.

She appeared from belowdecks and handed him a Windbreaker. He held it up to check the size.

"It should fit. It's a man's jacket," she said.

He arched a brow. "Oh, yeah?"

"It's my father's. He used to sail with me before he and Mom moved to Idaho."

Oh, her adoptive father. Grady slipped on his dry shirt, then the jacket. "How are things with your parents? And… your biological father?"

Maddie's face lit up. "He's coming to watch me race. To watch us race."

"That's great."

"Yes and no. I'm terrified." Maddie struggled with her own Windbreaker, and Grady tugged it up and over her arms then shoulders.

Holding the collar, he leaned close and kissed her, lingering. "This is a good thing, isn't it?"

"I know. It's just that I struggle sometimes with the fact that he knew about me but let me live a lie."

"Oh, Maddie…"

She pulled away from him. "Do you have any idea what it's like to believe something your whole life and then to find out that it was all a big lie? A big facade."

When she pressed her face into her hands, he stepped forward and tried to tug her to him. Dropping her hands, she stepped away, drew in a breath. "I'm okay."

He ducked his head a little. "You sure?"

"Yeah. I have to get over this. Let go and forgive. I want it behind me so I can get to know my father without this resentment crowding in. I'd really like to trust him. Trust anyone, for that matter." She lifted a shoulder. "Trust you, but this little voice inside my head keeps telling me that there's some dark secret that's going to ruin everything."

Grady stood frozen. Couldn't breathe. Couldn't swallow.

She gestured for them to raise the anchor, brushing aside the serious conversation. Funny she hadn't waited for him to answer. Hadn't expected one. Almost like she knew…she *knew,* that he was hiding something.

They raised the anchor and he hoisted the mainsail.

"You must think I have a lot of issues," she finally said.

"You've been hurt. Your reaction is normal." So much for laying it all out there. She didn't know him well enough, long enough, to trust him completely, but with her experience, a lifetime wouldn't be long enough.

How could he tell her about Taylor sending him here to protect her from the other guys on the crew? Now that he'd gotten to know them, he was pretty confident they were all great guys and wouldn't hurt Maddie, making Taylor's request absurd. In fact, Ricky had a girlfriend and treated Maddie more like a sister than a conquest. No, she was a conquest to Taylor.

Regardless, she might think Grady had toyed with her heart, or that their relationship had been based on a lie. At the very least, she'd think he was a jerk for betraying his friend.

And she would be right.

He recalled Bob's words when Grady had shared his dilemma. To be true to his word, he shouldn't give it lightly. Should be selective when giving it. Taylor wasn't exactly a guy trapped by enemy fire who was counting on Grady to save him. He was a guy who'd taken advantage of the fact that Grady owed him. Still, the blame belonged to Grady for agreeing to help in the first place.

But he *had* given his promise, so now what? He'd made a big mistake, and there were no easy answers. But one thing was for sure, Maddie would be the biggest casualty. She would be the one hurt the most.

Grady sat outside on the balcony and admired the stars. Taylor's condo was situated on the side facing away from the town, so the light pollution was minimal.

He considered his last conversation with Taylor. The guy hadn't even called him to find out how his interview had gone last week. Grady hoped his friend would consider his words about Maddie. Just let her go—she wasn't for him. The problem was that Grady couldn't exactly tell if his opinion in the matter was self-serving.

Maddie's words from their night together at the cove swam over him. *This little voice inside my head keeps telling me that there's some dark secret that's going to ruin everything.*

While the secret he kept wasn't exactly earth-shattering, her experiences compounded things. He hadn't been up front with her. That would be a huge transgression to Maddie, and she would never look at him the same after she knew the truth.

Hanging his head, he scraped his fingers over his scalp. *Lord, what do I do with this mess? How do I tell her the truth?*

And then his cell rang. It was Taylor. This time, he actually wanted to talk to his friend, though he dreaded the conversation.

A bat darted a few yards in front of him, searching for insects in the night air. He answered the call. "Hey."

"How'd the interview go?" Taylor's flat tone conveyed his mood.

He hadn't liked what Grady had had to say during their last conversation, that was obvious. Likely, he didn't even care about the interview, only wanted information about Maddie.

Grady shared the details and explained that though he'd remain hopeful, he knew he couldn't stop the job search. "Don't put all your eggs in one basket, my grandpa used to say."

"Yeah, my sentiments exactly. That's why I didn't turn Cindy away. She's my sister's friend and she offered to help out when Susan was at work, okay? Turns out she likes me.

And I like her, too." Taylor blew out a breath. "Listen, I've been thinking about our last conversation."

Pressing back against the seat, Grady blew out a breath. *Here it comes.* "What about it?"

"You said that Maddie had found someone."

"Yeah, I did. But what does that matter, because so have you."

"Who is it?"

Squeezing his eyes, Grady gripped the chair. Again, what did that matter, considering Taylor's Colorado interest? But unfortunately it did matter. Grady searched for the right words.

"It's you, isn't it?"

"Taylor…"

"You're falling for her." Taylor hadn't asked Grady. It was a simple statement.

His friend had been able to read that over the phone?

"You." Then Taylor released a string of words Grady never thought he'd hear. He never thought he'd be a person who deserved to hear them. "I trusted you. I have a lot of friends, and you were the only one I knew I could trust. I can't believe how wrong I was. And you were always so proud of yourself with your 'I'm a man of my word' stuff."

Grady let Taylor go on until he'd finished. Then finally, he replied, "You're right. I messed up. I should never have agreed to this farce, and I wouldn't have had I known you'd be playing the field while you were in Colorado. No wonder you stayed there so long when you could be here with Maddie—the girl you claim you care about."

"Dude, none of that matters. A friend doesn't steal another friend's girl."

"Okay, so here's the thing. She wasn't into you. She *isn't* into you. She was never your girl." Had he really just said that?

Taylor burst out laughing. "I can't believe we're fighting over a girl."

Grady frowned, nausea making his stomach roil. He and Taylor had been friends for too long for this to actually be happening. He couldn't believe it had come to this.

"Okay, I have to know this. Did you kiss her?"

Why'd he have to ask? "Can you just let this go?"

"You mean can I just let her go because she's not into me anyway?"

"There is that."

"No, I cannot let this go, Grady. What would your grandpa think about you now, huh? You're moving to California anyway, so what do you care? You never planned to stay in Crested Butte. If anyone is doing her wrong, it's you. If anyone needs to let her go, it's you, Grady. You've betrayed me, you've betrayed yourself and in the end you'll betray Maddie. If you earn her trust and then run off to Cali, you'll break her. You know that, right?"

Grady squeezed his eyes shut, steeling himself against the pain as Taylor drove the words deep and then twisted.

"Now tell me that's not the truth."

"I...can't."

"That's right. You can't."

"But in answer to your question about what my grandpa would say? I can tell you this. My grandpa would say that a friend shouldn't call in a favor on a girl and then go cheat on the girl he's trying to get."

Taylor sighed long and hard, then chuckled. "Oh, man."

Grady thought Taylor almost sounded like he was sorry.

"If you weren't planning on taking that California job," Taylor said, "and you knew you were going to stay there with Maddie, then I'd walk away. But if they offer you the job, you have to take it. You have no choice. And you don't have anything to offer Maddie if you stay. So I'm coming back to my condo, and I have every intention of staying there long enough to woo her, or whatever it is that women call it. You and me are friends, and I called dibs on Maddie, and I'm the one who's staying. You are the one who is walking away."

What were they? In high school?

Taylor made good points. All of them true. Grady couldn't think straight. A sharp pain jabbed in his head. He rubbed his temples, admitting to himself that he shouldn't have acted on the feelings he had for Maddie. He had nothing to offer her. No future. The one thing he'd thought he had—integrity—he'd lost. And that seemed to be the very thing she needed most. If the regatta wasn't a few days away, he'd leave, because no matter what he did, he would hurt Maddie. She counted on him for this regional regatta. Not only her, but Cameron, Lance and Ricky, too.

He'd help Maddie win, if he could. In that one thing, he wouldn't let her down.

Chapter 16

Maddie steered the *Crescent Moon* into the marina and the crew lowered and tied the sails. Once the boat was moored in the slip, everyone stepped onto the pier. She couldn't help but notice the frown lines edging the faces of each person.

"Too much traffic out there today." Ricky rubbed his neck.

"That was nothing compared to how race day will be," Cameron said.

Lance chuckled. "Well, this isn't my first time around the lake in a race."

Maybe not, Maddie thought, but it was her first time competing against so many exceptional sailors, and in her small corner of the world.

"Come on, guys, my father will be here to watch," she said. "That's stress enough for me, but we can't let the pressure get to us."

"We knew competitors would get here a few days early

to sail the lake," Grady said. "We need to sail again tomorrow so we can get used to the increase in traffic."

If only that was the reason their sailing rhythm was off today. Grady glanced at the parking lot next to the marina like a guy who couldn't wait to get away. Sure enough, he pulled his keys out of his pocket.

"Back here tomorrow same time, or what?" He arched a brow, looking at Cameron, Ricky, Lance, and then a short-lived glance at Maddie.

"Sure," she said. "Same time."

After everyone voiced their agreement, Grady gave Maddie a weak nod, holding her gaze for less than a full second, but he told her something in that short time. Or at least she imagined he tried. What was it she'd seen in his eyes—regret?

"I'll see you tomorrow," he said.

Then he left her standing there and hurried up the pier back to his Mazda. She watched him until Ricky turned to her. "You coming, Mads?"

"I need to grab something from the boat," she said. "You go ahead."

Maddie hoped he didn't hear the despair in her voice.

Her longtime sailing friend studied her for a moment. If he noticed her emotional state, he didn't say anything. "Tomorrow."

Maddie hopped back aboard her keelboat and went below to the cabin. She retrieved her father's Windbreaker and plopped on the small bed, holding the jacket to her chest. Grady had worn this.

Funny how things could change so fast. The news about her birth father had left her stunned, had knocked her world off its axis. She'd vowed she'd never be blindsided like that again.

Fear curdled in her stomach—she had the feeling that

Grady was hiding something. That he was about to tell her some truth that would again rock her world. Why couldn't she just get over the lie she'd been forced to live? Why did it have to color everything in her life?

But even if Grady didn't have a secret that would leave Maddie broken, he'd kissed her and made her believe he cared for her in a deep way. That was enough to mess with her life.

She'd let him in, allowed his heart to tangle up with hers. Now he was pulling back, and it hurt in a million different ways that were impossible to put into words.

The kiss in the water had stayed with her. She couldn't get it out of her head, and she hadn't wanted to. Sailing had been everything to her until Grady had stepped into her world. The air smelled fresher, the buttes and mesas burned brighter in the desert sun and the lake shimmered with clarity.

The past couple of days had been like a dream—knowing that her father was coming to watch them sail, and a guy she believed she could trust had made her fall in love with him.

The thought caused her to gasp softly. Did she love him? *Oh, no...*

Squeezing her eyes, she brought the Windbreaker to her face and breathed in the scent Grady had left behind. Subtle, but there nonetheless.

After the kiss in the lake, he'd been distant on the phone. Though she couldn't explain it exactly, she could sense it. She hoped his aloofness had been the stress of searching for employment coupled with the pressure of sailing in a marginally big race—something Grady had never done— and had nothing at all to do with their budding relationship, though *budding* might not be the right word, considering her feelings had bloomed overnight.

But his detachment had followed him onto her boat

today, putting the crew's cohesiveness off because he had pulled away from Maddie emotionally. She'd been such an idiot to let him charm his way into her heart with his grin. His kisses. Him just being him.

The tears came. She hated crying, but the hurt inside was too much.

Her emotions finally spent, Maddie sat up and looked down at the jacket she'd wept into. Ugh. She'd have to wash it. Like Lindy had said when Maddie had cried into her blouse, the tears would come out in the wash. If only the rest of life's unwelcome moments could be so easily resolved.

She hoped another crying jag wasn't on the horizon. She could hate herself for letting the tears get the best of her, but she'd hate herself worse if she didn't face Grady to find out what was going on. He owed her an answer, and she wouldn't allow herself to become the victim of a broken heart or otherwise. At least not without explanation.

She couldn't sail in the race until she'd cleared the air. Why was he playing games?

The truth was all she wanted.

Grady slammed the door behind him and leaned against it, panting for breath.

How he hated running. That was exactly why he'd tortured himself with a five miler. He'd hoped the pain could draw out his hurt over what he was doing to Maddie. It would have been a temporary fix at best, if it had worked. But it hadn't.

He was on the verge of a monumental failure he could never have dreamed up—letting his best friend down, and crushing the heart of the woman he… Did he love her? He'd never been in love with anyone before, but Maddie—

she was everything he wanted. And that was why stepping away from her ripped him apart.

He grabbed a glass of water in the kitchen and chugged it down. Closing his eyes, he experienced once again the pain that had seared through him at the look in Maddie's eyes when he'd said goodbye that afternoon. Of course, she'd sensed that he'd eased back from their relationship. They'd grown so close so fast that he didn't have to move away much for her to feel the difference. He might as well have crossed a great chasm in one simple step. What mattered now was winning the race for her, and staying true to his friend. But if today's training practice was any indication, the rest of the crew had sensed the invisible rift between Grady and Maddie.

They would have lost the regatta if they'd sailed today. He ran more water in the glass and guzzled it down.

Someone knocked.

Groaning inside, Grady moved to the door and glanced through the peephole.

Maddie? His pulse jumped. This was bad.

Dripping with sweat, he probably wasn't presentable, but she'd seen him in this state before.

An ache swept through his chest—he hadn't expected to face her like this. With the race practically on them, all he needed to do was avoid her. Then his commitment would be done. They could both move on. No harm done.

Yeah, right. If only he hadn't fallen for her. Hadn't kissed her, held her in his arms.

Grady opened the door. "Maddie. What's up?" He was no good at injecting nonchalance into his voice.

Her beautiful smile went a long way to cover the slight swelling around her eyes, the red in the corners. But not far enough. His heart stuttered. *Please, God, please don't let me be the reason she has been crying.* He almost asked her what was wrong. Why she'd been crying, but the words were trapped in his brain.

She lifted her left shoulder. "Can we talk?"

He hated hearing how desperate she sounded. Opening the door wide, he gestured her inside. "Come in."

She dropped her purse on the sofa and faced him. She looked him up and down, a grin slipping onto her face. "Did you actually go running? I thought you hated to run."

"I do." Grady didn't want to stand too near, so he went back into the kitchen and stared at her from across the counter—a nice cold barrier between them would do the trick. Right. "Would you like something to drink?"

"No, thanks, I'm fine." Her smile dropped. "Grady, what's going on?"

Man, he wished he could shower off. Splash water on his face, at the very least. "What do you mean?"

"Really? You're going to pretend you haven't started jibing? Turning the other way?"

He huffed a laugh. "Yes, I thought I'd pretend that I don't know what you're talking about."

A smile tried to tear across her face at his attempt at levity, but a somber expression won out. "Just tell me the truth. I'm a big girl, you know? I want whatever is bothering you—if it's us, or something else—resolved and behind me so I can focus on the race."

"See, I told you we shouldn't have gotten involved. It's too much of a distraction."

"Is that what this is really about? That I'm a distraction for you? Or is there something else?"

How much should Grady tell her? He didn't want to ruin things for Taylor. Even though Grady didn't think Maddie was interested in his friend, or ever would be, it really wasn't his place to make that call. But telling her everything would seal that forever. If there was one thing

Grady knew about her, she didn't like to be controlled or manipulated, or lied to, whatever the reason, even if it were a simple omission. Taylor's scheme was everything Maddie hated. And Grady had been part of it.

"I'd really like to shower off first, if you don't mind. I was just heading that way when you knocked."

"Oh, no, you don't. You don't get time to figure out what you're going to say. When did telling the truth become so hard for you, Grady?"

"Fine. I'm sorry if I came across cold today. I'm just feeling bad about everything, that's all."

"Bad about everything? You're going to have to do better than that. Tell me what I need to know."

I care about you, Maddie. No, telling her that would make things more convoluted. And she'd accuse him of not acting like it.

"I'm planning to leave the day after the regatta. Or maybe even ten minutes after it's over. You know that. You've always known that."

"True enough. I guess I deluded myself into hoping you would change your mind."

"I won't." Even if Taylor wasn't in the picture, it wouldn't matter. "I know that I'm saying this again. I shouldn't have kissed you, and I'm sorry. Look at me, Maddie, I'm a complete failure. I don't have a job. I can't offer you anything. Getting involved, taking our relationship further, doesn't serve a purpose. I'm just trying to protect the both of us. I don't want to get hurt, do you?" Too late.

Pain flashed in her eyes.

The same way it did in the agonizing, throbbing beat of his own heart.

Chapter 17

Maddie practically ran down the steps from the condo. She'd heard enough. She shouldn't have run away—it made her look desperate and pathetic, but the pain had started behind her eyes. She'd wanted to be strong and unbreakable, and she'd built up a wall around her heart. She had barricaded herself in, but she hadn't been prepared for her reaction to Grady. What really got her was that he hadn't told her anything she didn't already know.

She just hadn't expected him to turn so cold so fast. To act this way.

When she reached her car, her face burned with the fresh, raw heat of hurt and anger spilling from her eyes. She thrust her hand up to swipe the tears away. Maybe no one would happen across her in the parking lot.

A hand gripped her arm and turned her around.

Grady clutched her shoulders. "Look at me."

She shut her eyes. "I don't want you to see me like this. Please, let me go."

"No. I need to see you. I feel the same way inside, I promise."

She opened her eyes. "Then why?"

"Taylor sent me here to sail in his place, yes, but there's another reason."

She edged away from him. "I'm listening."

Hanging his head, he blew out a breath. "I feel like I'm breaking a confidence, but I see no other way."

He looked at her again, regret drowning in his desert-sea eyes. "He likes you, Maddie. A lot. He wanted me to watch out for you. Make sure that Ricky or one of the other guys didn't step in where he left off. I guess maybe he thought he had something more going with you. Was afraid one of them would take you away. I was supposed to be a kind of placeholder, but obviously things got out of control. The thing is, Taylor asked me because he knew he could count on me. Could trust me. You know that's important to me, right? If a person doesn't have honor in everything they do, then nothing matters. I messed up, I know that. But I need for what's between you and me to be over before it's too late. I'm not going to be that person who can't be trusted. By Taylor. By anyone."

Maddie hoped the heat in her eyes would sear him. "What about me, Grady? You played me. You and Taylor both. You were the one person I thought I could trust. We got close, and now I find out Taylor sent you to play me. So, in fact, you're the person who can't be trusted by *me*."

"It's not like that, Maddie." Desperation cracked his voice. "That's not what he wanted from me, and I never would have agreed to use you like that. I care about you, and that's why I wanted you to know everything. Please… I'm sorry…. Can you ever forgive me?"

"You know how I hate being manipulated." Loathing seethed from her words. "I can't believe this is happening."

She opened her car door and sat in the driver's seat. "I don't ever want to see you again. Taylor, either."

Grady crouched down next to her, keeping her from shutting the door. "You have every right to say that. I'm so sorry about everything. But I'm not going to let you down on race day, I promise you that. Think about Ricky, Cameron and Lance. They deserve our best. Don't you want your father to see—"

"Don't you use him against me. Or use any of them against me." Maddie pressed her forehead against the steering wheel, willing the fury to die down.

He was right. She couldn't let him destroy her. She still had her little keelboat and the chance to win a regional regatta and her parents and her father and she had a future, obviously without Grady. Maybe she could go stay with her father in Connecticut for a while and forget about Grady and Taylor, about Desert Sea Gifts being sold out from under her.

Forget everything but sailing—her one true love. But it would be difficult. Ever since Grady had come into her life, she knew that sailing would never be enough again.

"Maddie?" he asked, the tenderness in his voice shooting right through her and reminding her of their kisses. If she could only forget being in his arms, of feeling cherished.

Why'd you have to do this to me? But she'd never voice the words, never show him how deeply he'd cut her. What kind of weak hull she must have to so easily sink.

"Just go, Grady."

Maddie wasn't sure how long she sat there with her head pressed against the steering wheel, but she needed to see straight before she drove anywhere. When she leaned back, Grady was gone. She'd bet he'd call Taylor immediately to warn him about what to expect from her if she called. It didn't matter, though. She planned to block Taylor's calls, at least for a while. If not forever.

That night, Maddie lay in her bed and stared at the ceiling. What was it about her that made people think they needed to go behind her back, manipulate her, protect her, whatever it was they called it?

Turning on her side, she watched the moonbeams filtering through the miniblinds and splaying across her maroon carpet. If only Taylor and Grady's charade didn't remind her so much of the way her parents had kept the truth from her. Sure, that lie was a much deeper deception that changed everything about who she thought she was. But on some level, Taylor and Grady's actions invoked the same feelings of betrayal in her. So why was she feeling sorry for Grady?

She gasped. That was what he'd meant. When she'd told him he must be grateful to Taylor for saving his life, Grady had replied, "You have no idea."

Grady *owed* Taylor.

Maddie sat up, boiling anger firing up her throat. That Taylor. How tough that must have been for Grady. No matter how hard she tried, she couldn't think of him as a jerk—someone who didn't care about people. She couldn't see him using her like so many others would have. He'd wanted to keep his word to his friend, that was all, but he'd fallen for her and betrayed everyone.

She fell back in the bed and smashed the pillow in her face. She couldn't feel for him—in the end, he'd sacrificed Maddie's trust. He'd sacrificed their relationship. What he *had* with her.

What he could have had with her.

Not unlike what her father had done.

* * *

The buzzing security light his only illumination, Grady jangled the keys in the door to his boat-repair garage and stepped inside. Musty oldness mingled with the smell of oil and gas and epoxy and fiberglass, wrapping him in memories of his grandfather. He had memories of his parents, too, but he'd been so young when they'd been killed that it was hard to remember them as well as his grandfather.

He breathed in the smells that somehow grounded him and brought him back to who he was. On the two-hour drive to Harris from Crested Butte, he'd thought he would suffocate. His complete failure to be a loyal and good friend to the two people he cared about most pinched his chest so he couldn't breathe. The way he'd hurt Maddie, the look in her eyes, had been too much—he'd had to get out of town.

He stood in the garage in the dark and listened to the symphony of insects and frogs outside. A dog barked in the distance. Other than that, he was alone. Kicking the door shut behind him, he found his way to the workbench in the corner and flipped on only a small lamp.

Grady gripped the counter and listened to Maddie's words in his head. Saw the look in her eyes, on her face. How had he let things become so completely distorted and out of control?

He'd only wanted to do the right thing.

Why, God, why?

Did he really have to fail at everything?

Grady picked up a mason jar filled with old nails and threw it across the garage. Hitting something hard in the dark corner, the jar shattered across the floor. Brilliant.

He lowered himself into the ancient chair that had belonged to his grandfather and leaned back, resting his head. He closed his eyes and thought back to that day on his mountain bike, riding the trails in Colorado. The crisp mountain air. Kurt was up ahead, and Grady meant to catch him, taking a switchback on the trail too fast. His tires had skidded and lost traction, and he'd gone over the cliff.

Grady pressed the heels of his palms into his eyes.

Once again, the rush of terror engulfed him as he plummeted. At some point, he'd called out to the Lord. He didn't remember much after that. Everything had gone black. Supposedly, he'd hit his head. Then drowned in the river.

He should have died. Taylor had revived him, though— gotten a pulse, forced the water from his lungs—and Grady had woken in the hospital with a concussion.

His grandfather had been there that day. Had traveled to Colorado to be with him. Grady's friend Kurt had told him about the guy who'd saved him, and Grady had wanted to meet him. He and Taylor had hit it off from the start. Their personalities had clicked, and Grady had soon realized he had a new friend. Then his grandfather had been the one to invite Taylor to come see them in Harris. To Grady's surprise, Taylor had done just that and decided to stay awhile.

What if Grady had gone on with his life and parted ways with the guy who had dragged him from the river that day?

He squeezed the bridge of his nose, reining in his thoughts. No. He couldn't blame this disaster on Taylor. Deep down, he was a good guy. He hadn't meant anything by his simple request from Grady. He'd be there to help Maddie with the race and keep an eye on things for Taylor at the same time. Neither of them had understood Maddie's struggle with trust, and how this might affect her.

A noise startled him. Someone knocked, opened the door. His heart jumping, Grady was on his feet.

Bob Lawrence. "Oh, it's you," Grady said, and sucked in a breath.

"Scared you?"

"Yeah. Wasn't expecting anyone. It's late." Grady half smiled, half frowned. "What are you doing here?"

"Saw the light on." The guy shut the door behind him and came in.

"Oh." That still didn't explain anything.

"Was driving by." He stuck his hands in his pockets. "Been considering buying this place for myself."

"You have?"

"Sure. It meant a lot to your grandfather. It means a lot to you. I don't have family to speak of. This could be good for me."

At the thought of someone else owning this business, Grady had realized how much he didn't want to part with it. But if it was Bob, then Grady could let go of it a little easier. It almost felt right—that maybe he hadn't done so much wrong.

Bob bent over and picked up a shard of glass. A question in his eyes, he glanced at Grady.

"I had to throw something."

"Want to talk about it?" Bob eased onto a stool.

What was he doing? Trying to take Grady's grandfather's place? The idea should have been offensive, but somehow Grady appreciated this man. Maybe that was because Bob appreciated Grady's grandfather, knew him in a way Grady never had.

Then…Grady told him everything.

Bob listened intently, nodding now and then to let Grady know he remained tuned in.

"I don't think my grandfather would be proud of me now," Grady said. "I've let him down in every way possible."

He stood, then walked to Grady and squeezed his shoulder. "Son, I promise you, your grandfather is proud of you right now from where he's watching behind those pearly gates. I'd be proud if you were my grandson. Don't be so hard on yourself. Besides, even if no one here on earth could give you their approval, you need to get your validation from God. He's the only one who matters. He won't ever lead you wrong."

Chapter 18

Maddie's palms grew moist as she stared out the window at the approaching regional jet. Her father was on that small plane.

She hated how nervous she'd become while waiting near the baggage claim in the Crested Butte Municipal Airport. Grady's betrayal had opened her wound just when she'd thought she had moved on. She'd brooded all night long over Grady and Taylor, over the fact that her birth father had given her up just like that—no matter the reasons. All of it pricking her heart like an arrow with a poisonous tip.

As the plane landed and taxied out of sight, she tried to push it all down once again. Put it behind her, something she thought she'd already done.

Trusting others had been too hard, and she reminded herself that her father wasn't someone she could count on, in the end. She shouldn't let down her guard like she'd done with Grady and Taylor. She shut her eyes—how had it come to this? How had she misjudged them?

When she opened her eyes, her gaze fell on the artwork decorating the walls. One familiar painting stood out—it was of a clipper anchored in a cove. The same print hung on the wall at Desert Sea Gifts, only the one at the gift shop included a Bible verse. What was it again?

We have this hope as an anchor for the soul, firm and secure, Hebrews 6:19.

Yes, that was the verse, but what was the hope?

And then she remembered: *I am your hope.*

The quiet answer calmed the waves battering her soul.

Drawing in a breath to steady her nerves, she reminded herself that she could count on God to be there for her always. The past was the past, and she wanted it to stay there. She needed to hoist her sails and go where God would take her, and to do that, she needed to forgive.

Help me to forgive, Lord.

She needed to smile at her father when she saw him. God had given them a second chance.

Her father entered the baggage-claim area and searched his surroundings. Before she could call out his name or get his attention, he saw her.

Smiling, Maddie hurried to him. The joy of seeing him helped bury her sullen thoughts. He opened his arms and she rushed in. She breathed in his musky, familiar scent and suddenly she was a little girl again—*his* little girl again. A long-lost memory surfaced, and Maddie remembered her father. This father.

Maddie fought back the tears. *No, don't cry, don't cry.* He was her father, yes, but she had another father—the man who'd raised and loved her as his own. In that way, she was blessed beyond measure. When he released her, she blinked away unshed tears and once again smiled at him.

"I can't believe you're here," she said.

"It's good to see you again, Maddie. I'm glad you agreed

to let me watch you in the regatta. You'll do great, I'm sure." He pressed his hand against the small of her back to urge her over to where people had already gathered to collect their luggage. "After all, you're my daughter."

Maddie couldn't help the way his last words affected her and, though she'd wanted to appear like everything was wonderful, her shoulders slouched. Her father grabbed his luggage and Maddie led him to her Outback in the parking lot. The hotels in Crested Butte and the surrounding towns were mostly booked for the regatta, but Lindy and her husband had a guest room they had offered to Maddie's father. She'd take him to dinner first, then she planned to head to bed early.

Before she turned on the ignition, he put his hand on hers to stop her. "Wait. Is there something wrong?"

She smiled and faced him. "Of course not. Why do you ask?"

He squeezed her hand. "A person doesn't have to know you long to see that something's bothering you. That's it, isn't it?"

"What are you talking about?"

"That I haven't known you long. That I wasn't there for you, a part of your life." He scraped a hand down his face and looked out the passenger window. "That...we didn't tell you."

"We talked about this already." Maddie considered whether she should simply start the car and drive. She moved her hand away from the ignition. "But I guess not enough. I'm trying to forget all that, but it's hard. Every time someone lies to me, it sends me right back to the lie I've lived my whole life."

Her breaths came a little quicker. *Don't cry, don't cry. Keep control of your emotions. This situation. Your life....*

He sighed and turned to face her again. "We had friends

that divorced. Two sets of friends, actually. It was devastating to their kids. Tore them up more when they used the kids to manipulate each other."

His gaze searched for understanding in hers, and she looked away.

He held her hand tighter. "So when the worst happened and your mother and I divorced, and then she remarried, we did what we thought was best for you at the time. I see now that we made a mistake. But it would have been hard on you to go back and forth between us. Confusing, when you were younger. It wasn't that I didn't want to see you, it was that I loved you so much I made the sacrifice to give you what I thought would be the best life. The years went by far too quickly, and then when I realized how things would affect you as an adult, it was too late. I've been praying for a chance to make things right. Please give me that chance."

The breath rushed from Maddie. She played with the car keys as she fought for composure.

"Maddie, listen to me. I need you to have some grace here. As much as I'd love to think I have it all figured out and a good grip on things, half the time I don't have a clue what I'm doing. We just can't control our lives that way. We're better off holding on to things loosely. Nothing belongs to us except our relationship with God."

She studied him then, his eyes filled with compassion and understanding. She wanted to return those sentiments. "I know. I just needed to hear that from you, I guess."

Grinning, he tugged her to him for a quick hug. "Then let's get some dinner inside you. You need your sleep. Tomorrow's a big day. When you race, just remember to—"

"Hold on loosely." Maddie didn't bother telling her father there was much more bringing her down. This was the first time her father had come to New Mexico to see her. It meant everything, and she didn't want to ruin it.

Winning would be good, but racing tomorrow, for him, meant everything. Grady Stone... He meant nothing.

If only it were true.

Grady arrived at the marina early enough to beat most of the spectators, but things were already busy as competing crews readied their vessels. He wished he and Maddie would have had the chance to work things out before they had to sail today. That last practice—when he'd let the guilt weigh on him—hadn't been their best. Everything was somehow thrown off. He hated going into this with conflict between them, but he was willing to put it aside to give his all and win. The race was psychological as much as it was anything else. If they went into this with thoughts of accepting less than victory, then they had already lost. Every move, every decision made, had to be certain. Had to be aggressive.

Maddie didn't like to be controlled or manipulated, and he couldn't blame her for that. It was because of her need to be in control, to be certain, that she made such a great skipper. Grady's argument with her couldn't have come at a worse time, though. The big question—could Maddie put things behind them for the race? If not, there wasn't any chance they'd win. As their skipper, she had to maintain control of herself, her crew and her boat. Nothing outside of that could distract her.

Though...Maddie wasn't some robot that could simply forget about what Grady had done—even for a day. What an idiot he'd been. He'd told her after that first kiss they couldn't afford this distraction.

Oh, boy. They were in trouble.

If only he could make her understand that he hadn't

meant to hurt her. A hand gripped Grady's arm and yanked him around. He was surprised to see Taylor staring back at him, leaning on his crutches.

"Taylor!" Grady wasn't sure whether to give him a bear hug or not, but the guy's scowl warned him.

His friend ground out his words. "What did you tell her?"

Grady held up his palms. "This is not the time or the place. She's counting on me to help her win."

"She wouldn't even talk to me, Grady. What happened?"

"Things just got out of hand. She wanted answers and I tried to explain. She doesn't trust either one of us now."

And hearing those words impaled him for a million reasons. Because he loved her. Yes, he loved her. He'd known it for a while.

Taylor stared at him, his jaw tight. Grady couldn't exactly share that news with his best friend, and, oh, he hated that. How had it come to this? *God, help me.* "Don't worry. We'll work this out. We'll make her understand, okay?"

"How, Grady? Tell me how."

"Look, can we talk about this later?"

Repositioning his crutches, Taylor turned away and left him. In the distance, Grady saw Maddie change course, skirting around the parking lot to avoid the both of them, though she'd have to face Grady soon enough on her boat. Part of him wondered if she'd somehow replaced him overnight. Considering the depth of their betrayal of her, he wouldn't be surprised.

If only his grandpa were still alive, maybe he could have given Grady advice and kept him out of this situation from the beginning. Likely the boat-repair business would be thriving and Grady would be working. He wouldn't be available to sail in Taylor's place and betray his friend. He wouldn't have met Maddie and...fallen in love.

He wouldn't have destroyed her trust or lost her before he even had her.

Grady scraped his emotions off the asphalt and headed for Maddie and her boat. He needed to put his best self forward, just as he'd done in his interviews. Set his mind to think positive.

Appear enthusiastic.

Project certainty.

Though it was the hardest thing he'd ever done, he turned his thoughts to sailing the race of his life and let everything else go.

Chapter 19

Starting a race in a sailboat was tricky because they couldn't just sit and wait for the gun to go off. Fortunately, Maddie had practiced starting with her crew enough times that she had a good sense of how to hit the starting line at a favorable tack and speed, and at just the right moment. Crossing the invisible line before the signal meant a restart for the race, or turning around and sailing across the line again—and that would mean lost time.

Seventy boats sailed back and forth hoping to maneuver into a starting position at precisely the right moment. Maddie had practiced, but she hadn't experienced competing for a good position with so many boats. She didn't like the way these newcomers to her lake jockeyed, but she could be aggressive, too.

When you broke things down, only two things mattered. Sailing as fast as you could across the shortest distance. Maneuvering and manipulating the competition was next.

At the bow, Grady's voice rang out strong and sure as he counted down the prestart, and it sent an unwanted pang through her. She needed to throw off the blanket of hurt covering her, because Grady was on board for the length of this regatta. She couldn't change that now.

When he got to thirty seconds, her jittery nerves would tighten, the tension on her boat would become palpable. But it was a good and necessary tension that would melt away as her crew operated like well-greased gears that fit together perfectly.

Then it wouldn't matter if a few things weighed on her mind. At least she hoped and prayed it wouldn't matter. Her sailing-champion father was here to watch her.

Maddie couldn't believe this day had finally come. Hadn't she prepared for this her whole life? Well, maybe not, but she felt as if everything in her life was culminating at this place, this event. Her complicated relationships were all tied up in this race—but she didn't need to think about them today.

She lifted her face to the sun, thankful for the warm day. The winds were a light ten-knot breeze, but strong winds were predicted for later. With so many boats nearing the starting line, the lake was noisy. She'd worked out hand signals for the crew, and especially her bowman, which meant she'd have to watch Grady all day. And, of course, she'd watch him—they were all ultra-aware of each other's every move in order to sail this boat.

As the *Crescent Moon* sailed windward on a starboard tack, Grady counted down until finally the gun went off, and Maddie's J24 crossed the starting line.

"Yes!" Maddie pumped her arm.

"Okay, boys, let's find the free wind today and just keep moving!" she shouted over the chaos of so many boats.

They sailed through a line of boats toward the windward mark, while other boats went left or right. The wind shifted hard to the right, and Maddie's crew left most of the fleet behind. With free air, they tacked as needed to maintain the lead. Her heart soared with the sails high in the mast as they rounded the windward mark ahead of the pack, but the day had only just started, and she still had ample opportunity to lose.

When Grady glanced back at her from the bow, his expression was somber. How many times had she seen him look back at her wearing his heart-stopping grin? She wished that she could erase everything that caused his frown and her pain. His dark eyes pleaded with her to understand. To forgive and forget. If she wasn't careful, he would drift right through everything that had come between them.

Stop it, Grady.

She drove her attention back to the moment, to managing her team, exactly where it should be.

Her crew didn't have to be told when to shift from side to side to redistribute weight, and they moved together almost like one living organism. Cameron pulled the twings then slid to the cockpit and trimmed the mainsail as necessary. Lance trimmed the sails. Ricky controlled the tiller, and Maddie focused on racing tactics and directing her crew. And Grady managed the foredeck with precision.

They'd successfully rounded the windward mark, but then hit a head tide, which slowed them down. Maddie glanced behind her to see that the rest of the fleet had caught up with them.

She'd lost her lead. By the time they were downwind near the leeward mark, Maddie still hadn't figured out how she would gain an advantage, and then a strong current swept the entire fleet toward the leeward mark.

Grady called out from the bow. She couldn't make out

his words, but looked where he pointed. A pack of sailboats headed toward the mark from the wrong side, and
the *Crescent Moon* would be caught up in their sweep if
Maddie didn't do something now.

Too many thoughts vied for position. In her gut, she
knew she had to think out of the box for this. She thought
back to the few words of advice her father had given her.

Sometimes winning the race requires reducing speed.

"Trim the sails." She hadn't believed him, but she could
see it in her mind now. "Douse the spinnaker!"

Ricky stared at her. "What are you doing?"

"Get it down now." She couldn't believe he would question her.

With the spinnaker collapsed, the *Crescent Moon*
slowed considerably, and the mass of boats behind them
passed them by.

"Great, that's just great." Ricky's angry tone startled
her.

"Just wait, will you? I didn't want to get caught up in
that mess," she said. "Get ready."

Many of the boats that had sailed by the *Crescent Moon*
were now swept to the wrong side of the mark. Others
rounded the mark too wide. That would cost them all time.

The confusion and chaos left a big hole.

Now...now they needed to raise the sails again. Her
crew worked together perfectly to alter their course in
order to cut through the gap the other boats left, bearing
away until the mainsail jibed and, on the tack, filled with
wind. Then they set the spinnaker again, which instantly
filled with free air, sending the *Crescent Moon* flying at
a nice clip. They gained an advantage once again.

She eyed Ricky.

"I'm sorry, okay?" He averted his gaze.

Grady had his back to her, and he moved like a man with purpose. True to his word—at least on this point—he'd given his all while sailing today. He'd been the one to alert her. They worked so well together, and she hated what had happened with their relationship. His words came back to her. *It's not like that, Maddie. I care about you, and that's why I wanted you to know everything. Please... I'm sorry.... Can you ever forgive me?*

Maybe she could forgive him, but in the end, he planned to leave anyway. In the end, there was nothing between them.

They moved from starboard to port to balance the boat, and Ricky lost his footing.

Then the wind made a radical shift. "I need that sail trimmed!"

Grady glanced back at her, and with Ricky down—had he twisted his ankle or something?—Grady moved to the sail at the same time as Maddie. They started trimming the boom. Before she could tell him to get back to his position, he leaned in.

"I love you, Maddie."

"What?"

"I know my timing stinks, but I need you to know."

"Watch out!" Someone hailed them from another boat approaching fast from only two boat lengths away leeward.

"What are you doing?" Maddie shouted the question, but she knew exactly what was happening. The *Crescent Moon* was windward and slightly ahead, and Nielsen figured he'd cut her off, force her to slow with the threat of collision.

She'd been momentarily stunned, but *she* had the right-of-way and wasn't about to give in. To Maddie's horror, Nielsen's boat overlapped with hers on the leeward side.

"The boom!" Grady called out.

Everything happened in slow motion. He shoved Maddie back and out of the way. Nielsen's boat collided with their boom, whipping it back and into Grady, then sweeping him overboard.

She heard her crew shouting "man overboard" and maybe she heard herself, too.

Nielsen swept by them, and unless he was disqualified for his unjustified hail and dangerous maneuver, he'd win. Maddie didn't care.

"Heave to!" She leaned over the boat. "Grady!"

He floated facedown in the water. Not good. Thank goodness he always insisted on wearing a lifejacket. "I'm going in after him."

Ignoring the protests of her crew, who volunteered to pull Grady in, Maddie jumped into the water and swam to him. She held him about the shoulders and swam back toward the boat as her crew tacked leeward, keeping her and Grady on the windward side. The boat drew near and Lance dropped the jib, stopping the boat.

Water lapped around them, reminding her once again of their kiss in the lake.

"He's hurt," she said, her voice shaky to her ears. "A gash on his head. And…I'm not sure he's even breathing."

Her whole body trembled with the fear of losing him. This was one situation she couldn't hope to control, but she knew someone who could. *Oh, God, please, I give control of my life to You, just…please…save Grady.*

"It'll be all right, Maddie," Ricky said.

Lance and Cameron hoisted Grady onto the deck, and Ricky helped Maddie up. Lake water dripping everywhere, Maddie watched as Lance opened Grady's life jacket.

"He must have hit his head and—"

Drowned? "No!" Maddie crouched next to Lance, and together they performed CPR, doing compressions and breathing to force the water from his lungs. "Grady, you are not going to leave me. You are going to wake up. Come on, Grady. Come on."

God, please, I want the chance to tell him how I feel, too. Please, save him.

Grady choked and coughed up water, rolling to the side. He groaned and blinked. "My head."

"You're alive," Maddie said through tears. "You're going to be all right."

Thank You, God.

He squinted up at her, a purple knot growing on his forehead. "What makes you think that?"

Maddie couldn't help herself. She leaned in and kissed him long and hard.

Grady had saved her. He'd taken the boom himself and saved her.

Taylor's condo felt uninviting as Grady nursed his headache, slouched on the sofa. But he couldn't go anywhere for a couple of days with a serious concussion. His thoughts were scrambled, and he couldn't concentrate or focus long enough to carry on a conversation with himself, much less anyone else.

That was why he was still reeling that he'd just accepted a job offer with Dynamics Corporation. It was like a dream come true. They weren't expecting him out there for another two weeks, so he'd have time to get over this headache. *Please, God...*

He closed his eyes and thought back to the race. Unfortunately, he couldn't recall that much about it, only a vague and disturbing memory.

Had he told Maddie he loved her? Or just dreamed that up? It was true enough, but he wasn't sure if he'd told her. He barely remembered her kiss on the boat, the pain in his head overshadowing that very important moment. She'd mostly been with him at the hospital when they'd checked him over and given him a prescription, but again, the pain had been all consuming.

And now here he sat, numb with drugs.

The door flew open and Taylor entered on his crutches, followed by Maddie, who was loaded down with a few grocery bags. She set them in the kitchen, then rushed by Taylor to sit next to Grady.

"How's your head?"

He winced. Her words sliced through him, compounding the pain. Sound, noise and light had that effect on him, even with the drugs. "I'm alive."

She squeezed his hand. He glanced up at her silvery-gray eyes. Beautiful eyes. Had she forgiven him? She was sitting here in Taylor's condo with the both of them, so yeah, she'd probably gotten over everything. But where did he stand with her?

How could he ever find out with Taylor hovering? Oh, yeah, it was Taylor's condo. And technically, Grady had only come here to help Taylor. His next step was to end this, to be the friend he'd promised to be.

"Dynamics called," he said. It was all he could do to get it out. "I got the job I wanted."

"You're moving?" Maddie's voice sounded distant.

Grady's thoughts twisted with heartache, splitting him open. He leaned his head back against the sofa, and the next thing he knew, he woke with a cold rag over his eyes. His head felt a little better as he slowly lifted it. The rag fell away.

"Where'd Maddie go?" he asked of no one in particular.

Taylor exited the hallway. "Dude, you fell asleep and she left."

Seriously? "Oh," he said, then huffed.

And…Taylor sounded like his old self. That was probably because Grady had officially removed himself from the situation.

Taylor came all the way into the living room and plopped into his La-Z-Boy. How many nights had Grady sat there and stared across the room at Maddie's picture on the empty bookshelf?

"Listen, Grady. We're friends. We're always going to be friends. No girl is going to come between us."

Sounded great, except for one thing: Maddie *had* come between them. "You need to speak slow and plain, like I'm five, okay?"

Taylor chuckled. "Maddie's into you. I knew it before I left Colorado, but I just couldn't stand to think that you'd bested me over a girl."

"I didn't best you. I told her I was leaving. I…let her go."

"You're an idiot. Why would I want her when she clearly loves you? Why would you just let her go?"

"I'm nothing if I can't be trusted."

"You don't remember, do you?"

Grady stared. "That depends."

"She told me what happened. Right after you told her that you loved her, that Nielsen character's boat collided with yours. You put yourself in harm's way for her. How can I compete with that?"

Oh, so he *had* told her how he felt. She must be as confused as he was. "No need to compete. I'm out of it now. I'm leaving."

But the words sounded wrong. His heart wasn't so sure they were true.

"Well, you got the wrong end of a very bad deal. I'm sorry I asked that favor of you, but I had no idea you two would hit it off so well."

Taylor stood and closed the distance, reaching out his

hand to clasp Grady's, and squeezed long and hard. "We're friends for life, deal?"

"Deal." Grady struggled to absorb everything Taylor had said, everything that had happened over the past twenty-four hours. He had assumed they hadn't won the race, but somehow that no longer mattered. Maddie hadn't mentioned it, either.

Taylor grinned. "Now I'm going to do you a big favor, because that's what friends are for."

"What's that?" Grady was ready to quit talking, thinking. But that wouldn't stop his heart from aching. How could he give Maddie up? And did he even have to? Why had he confessed his love for her only to walk away? Taylor was right—he was an idiot.

"I'm going to give you some friendly advice."

Maddie waited in a booth at Taco Joe's while her father ordered for them at the counter. No matter how hard she tried, she couldn't get the image of Grady taking the boom for her and falling overboard. Of him lying on the deck breathless, lifeless.

And minutes before that Maddie had been angry with him, believing she couldn't trust him, just like she couldn't trust anyone with what was important. But what *was* important? Her need to be in control so she would never get hurt? No matter how hard she tried, she'd never been in control of her life. Obviously, it could be snatched away from her at any moment. Someone she cared about could be snatched away, too.

So when she'd had the chance to face off with Taylor as they'd waited for Grady at the hospital, she'd told him that she'd had a change of heart. She knew that he'd never meant to harm her, and neither had Grady.

It seemed kind of strange to think of those two guys

fighting over her. Maddie had decided to let go and forgive Taylor and Grady. Her father and parents. God had blessed her with so much. He'd given her people who cared about her and wanted her in their lives.

Her father slid into the padded seat across from her and handed over her triple-chocolate shake. Maddie realized they were at the same booth where she had sat with Grady when they had eaten here. She hadn't been paying attention or she would have sat on the other side of the restaurant. No point in making an issue of that now in front of her father.

She and her father talked about the regatta and everything that had gone wrong. As tactician, Maddie blamed herself. She'd been distracted by Grady, no sense in her hiding the truth.

I love you, Maddie.

She wouldn't blame him for his poor timing, but she struggled to determine if his confession had caused the accident where he saved her and almost died. The regatta had continued on without the *Crescent Moon* and Nielsen had been disqualified. Another day of racing, and some team from San Diego had won and was now headed to the nationals.

"I'm sorry you came all this way and things ended like this." Maddie couldn't look at her father. "I wanted to win for you. Wanted you to see—"

"Maddie, stop." He reached across the table and pressed his hand over hers. "I'm sorry about the race. Those things happen, so you have to pick yourself up and keep going."

She'd placed her dreams on that regatta, hoping that when her father saw how well she could sail, she'd somehow be worthy of him. After a moment, she edged her gaze up to meet the intensity in his eyes.

"I didn't want you to be disappointed in me." *I wanted to make you proud.*

Her father shook his head. "You don't have to prove anything to me. I already know what an awesome sailor you are."

"Right." She gave a half smile. "Because I'm your daughter. How could I be anything less than a great sailor?"

He frowned. "No, Maddie. When I said that to you before, I was only teasing. I've been following your career— the postings about your wins on the local newspaper website. But none of that matters. You're my daughter and you don't have to be a great sailor for me to love you."

Had she needed to secure his love and thought she could if she had won the race? She allowed his words to sink in, wanting to believe them, to chase away the doubts hiding in the shadows. "Thanks. I needed to hear that one more time, I guess."

"Maddie." Her father's voice grew serious. "I came to New Mexico to see you, and to see you race in the regatta, but mostly I wanted to talk to you about something in person. I've been thinking about this for a while."

Oh, here it comes. "What is it?"

"I've wanted to make up for lost time ever since I gave you up. How about you come back with me? I have plenty of room. You could come and go as you please. Get a job, work for me or spend your time sailing with me."

"Oh, Daddy," she said. Wow, she said the *D* word. She couldn't think of anything she'd wanted more since learning about him. Getting to know him. Except.

I love you, Maddie. What was she supposed to do with that? Grady was moving to California. He'd told her that, in effect, letting her go.

Tears surfaced at the corner of her eyes. She blinked them away before her father could see. "I'd love to. When do we leave?"

Then…Grady walked through the door and sucked all

the oxygen from the room. He didn't approach the counter to order, but searched the room, his eyes landing on her.

"Go to him."

Maddie glanced back at her father. He nodded and smiled. "Go on. Go talk to him."

"But…"

"No buts, Maddie. This guy obviously cares about you, and you him. It's all over your face."

Torn between her father and Grady, Maddie hesitated. But then again, Grady had already said goodbye, hadn't he?

Her father leaned in. "I'll catch you later."

He slid from the booth.

"No." She reached for him.

He nodded, gesturing toward Grady.

Grady just stood there and stared, as though waiting for an invitation. Her father passed him and clapped him on the back, forcing Grady into taking a step forward. She glanced down at the table and waited for him to slide into the booth across from her.

Instead, he sat next to her and scooted closer. Pinned in, Maddie slid away from him and nearer to the wall.

"What are you doing here?" she asked.

"This." He cupped her face with his hands and kissed her, sending her mind and heart sailing, as if she were the spinnaker and Grady the wind, strong and sure and high in the mast.

He ended the sweet kiss softly, edging away, but then covered her lips with more soft kisses.

"I don't understand, Grady."

"I don't, either. I came here to kiss you for maybe the last time, depending on your reaction."

"And?"

"I've been a failure at so many things, Maddie, and I

know I really messed things up between us, but I can't let this fail. I can't let us fail, what we have. I won't. That is, if you feel the same way."

She tilted her head, sensing the burning glow she thought she'd feel if she'd won the regatta. "Grady, do you remember what you told me just before…"

"I love you, Maddie." He kissed her again.

"I saved your life, you know," she said, fighting the teasing grin that had erupted on her face.

"Yeah, right after I saved yours, sort of."

"I'm sorry it took almost losing you to see how much you mean to me. I think I knew all along, and that's why it hurt so much."

He squeezed her hands and brought them to his heart. "Feel how sorry I am for that."

She giggled. "Since I saved your life and you saved mine, sort of, maybe you owe me by sticking around to see if things work out."

He grinned. "I can do better than that."

Grady pulled a little antique box out of his pocket. "Maddie, will you marry me?"

Stunned by his proposal, Maddie palmed her mouth.

"It was my grandmother's. I found it in my apartment above the garage, and I knew if this moment came, I'd need it."

Maddie glanced out the pane-glass window to see her father standing in the parking lot watching. Grinning, he lifted his soda in a toast and nodded. And he'd only moments before invited her to stay with him, sail with him.

"Maddie?" Grady asked, his voice shaky.

She turned her attention back to this man she could never get out of her head or heart. And she didn't want to. "But…what about your job? California? You told me that you were leaving."

"You once told me that if staying close was important, I could find a way. And I will, if it means being with you." He scrunched up his face. "Besides, why would that keep us apart? We can go, or we can stay. But whatever we do, we do it together. I want to be your bowman forever. Or mast man, whatever you need. Only I want to do those things as your husband."

"Maybe sometime we can go see my father in Connecticut and sail with him."

Grady's cheek twitched. "What if we couldn't go, Maddie? Would you still want me? Would you still marry me?"

"Oh, Grady, yes. Yes, I'll marry you. As long as I'm with you, then it doesn't matter."

He gave a nervous laugh. "You had me worried there. I've never proposed before."

Maddie hugged him to her. She hadn't dreamed that she could feel this way about someone. That Grady would mean so much to her.

Her father stepped into view.

"So, are congratulations in order?" His deep, rich voice wrapped around her.

How awesome was God to script this moment so that the father she'd missed her whole life could be here to witness her engagement. She and Grady slipped from the booth and Grady shook her father's hand.

"He asked me if he could propose to you." Her father's eyes crinkled as he glanced between them.

"You did?" She stared at Grady, and then back to her father. "But didn't you just ask me to move to Connecticut with you to spend time with you?"

"Yes. I won't lie to you, I wanted that time with you. But I also wanted to put it out there so you could choose what was more important to you now, before things got too involved. Though I know I can trust you with this guy."

At her father's compliment, Grady's eyes brimmed with gratitude. Maddie loved witnessing his reaction. There wasn't anything more important to Grady.

And there wasn't any moment she treasured more than this one, standing here with these two men in her life—if she'd had any control, they wouldn't have been here. But thank goodness she couldn't control much of anything. Only God could. Everything had worked out as it should have because *all* things worked together for good for those who loved God.

Knowing that, Maddie's world would never be shaken to the core again.

Be my anchor, Lord.

* * * * *

REQUEST YOUR FREE BOOKS!

2 FREE INSPIRATIONAL NOVELS
PLUS 2
FREE
MYSTERY GIFTS

Love Inspired

YES! Please send me 2 FREE Love Inspired® novels and my 2 FREE mystery gifts (gifts are worth about $10). After receiving them, if I don't wish to receive any more books, I can return the shipping statement marked "cancel." If I don't cancel, I will receive 6 brand-new novels every month and be billed just $4.74 per book in the U.S. or $5.24 per book in Canada. That's a savings of at least 21% off the cover price. It's quite a bargain! Shipping and handling is just 50¢ per book in the U.S. and 75¢ per book in Canada.* I understand that accepting the 2 free books and gifts places me under no obligation to buy anything. I can always return a shipment and cancel at any time. Even if I never buy another book, the two free books and gifts are mine to keep forever.

105/305 IDN F49N

Name	(PLEASE PRINT)
Address	Apt. #
City	State/Prov.	Zip/Postal Code

Signature (if under 18, a parent or guardian must sign)

Mail to the Harlequin® Reader Service:
IN U.S.A.: P.O. Box 1867, Buffalo, NY 14240-1867
IN CANADA: P.O. Box 609, Fort Erie, Ontario L2A 5X3

**Are you a subscriber to Love Inspired books
and want to receive the larger-print edition?
Call 1-800-873-8635 or visit www.ReaderService.com.**

* Terms and prices subject to change without notice. Prices do not include applicable taxes. Sales tax applicable in N.Y. Canadian residents will be charged applicable taxes. Offer not valid in Quebec. This offer is limited to one order per household. Not valid for current subscribers to Love Inspired books. All orders subject to credit approval. Credit or debit balances in a customer's account(s) may be offset by any other outstanding balance owed by or to the customer. Please allow 4 to 6 weeks for delivery. Offer available while quantities last.

Your Privacy—The Harlequin® Reader Service is committed to protecting your privacy. Our Privacy Policy is available online at www.ReaderService.com or upon request from the Harlequin Reader Service.
We make a portion of our mailing list available to reputable third parties that offer products we believe may interest you. If you prefer that we not exchange your name with third parties, or if you wish to clarify or modify your communication preferences, please visit us at www.ReaderService.com/consumerschoice or write to us at Harlequin Reader Service Preference Service, P.O. Box 9062, Buffalo, NY 14269. Include your complete name and address.

LIDIR13R

REQUEST YOUR FREE BOOKS!

2 FREE INSPIRATIONAL NOVELS
PLUS 2
FREE
MYSTERY GIFTS

Love Inspired
HISTORICAL
INSPIRATIONAL HISTORICAL ROMANCE

YES! Please send me 2 FREE Love Inspired® Historical novels and my 2 FREE mystery gifts (gifts are worth about $10). After receiving them, if I don't wish to receive any more books, I can return the shipping statement marked "cancel." If I don't cancel, I will receive 4 brand-new novels every month and be billed just $4.74 per book in the U.S. or $5.24 per book in Canada. That's a savings of at least 21% off the cover price. It's quite a bargain! Shipping and handling is just 50¢ per book in the U.S. and 75¢ per book in Canada.* I understand that accepting the 2 free books and gifts places me under no obligation to buy anything. I can always return a shipment and cancel at any time. Even if I never buy another book, the two free books and gifts are mine to keep forever.

102/302 IDN F5CY

Name _____ (PLEASE PRINT) _____

Address _____ Apt. # _____

City _____ State/Prov. _____ Zip/Postal Code _____

Signature (if under 18, a parent or guardian must sign)

Mail to the Harlequin® Reader Service:
IN U.S.A.: P.O. Box 1867, Buffalo, NY 14240-1867
IN CANADA: P.O. Box 609, Fort Erie, Ontario L2A 5X3

Want to try two free books from another series?
Call 1-800-873-8635 or visit www.ReaderService.com.

* Terms and prices subject to change without notice. Prices do not include applicable taxes. Sales tax applicable in N.Y. Canadian residents will be charged applicable taxes. Offer not valid in Quebec. This offer is limited to one order per household. Not valid for current subscribers to Love Inspired Historical books. All orders subject to credit approval. Credit or debit balances in a customer's account(s) may be offset by any other outstanding balance owed by or to the customer. Please allow 4 to 6 weeks for delivery. Offer available while quantities last.

Your Privacy—The Harlequin® Reader Service is committed to protecting your privacy. Our Privacy Policy is available online at www.ReaderService.com or upon request from the Harlequin Reader Service.

We make a portion of our mailing list available to reputable third parties that offer products we believe may interest you. If you prefer that we not exchange your name with third parties, or if you wish to clarify or modify your communication preferences, please visit us at www.ReaderService.com/consumerschoice or write to us at Harlequin Reader Service Preference Service, P.O. Box 9062, Buffalo, NY 14269. Include your complete name and address.

LIHDIR13R

ReaderService.com

Manage your account online!
- Review your order history
- Manage your payments
- Update your address

**We've designed
the Harlequin® Reader Service
website just for you.**

Enjoy all the features!

- Reader excerpts from any series
- Respond to mailings and
  special monthly offers
- Discover new series available to you
- Browse the Bonus Bucks catalog
- Share your feedback

Visit us at:
ReaderService.com